THE NIM STORIES

THE NIM STORIES

WENDY ORR
PICTURES BY KERRY MILLARD

ALLEN&UNWIN
SYDNEY•MELBOURNE•AUCKLAND•LONDON

This paperback bind-up edition of *Nim's Island* and *Nim at Sea* published in 2013

Nim's Island first published in 1999
Nim at Sea first published in 2007
Nim's Island film tie-in edition published in 2008

Allen & Unwin
83 Alexander Street
Crows Nest NSW 2065
Australia
Phone: (61 2) 8425 0100
Fax: (61 2) 9906 2218
Email: info@allenandunwin.com
Web: www.allenandunwin.com

A Cataloguing-in-Publication entry is available from
the National Library of Australia
www.trove.nla.gov.au

ISBN 978 1 74331 649 8

Cover & text design by Sandra Nobes
Cover image by Pinnacle Films Inc
Cover design based on a poster by Pinnacle Films Inc
Hand lettering of title on cover by Geoff Kelly
Set in 11.5 pt Minion by Sandra Nobes
This book was printed in Feburary 2013 at McPherson's Printing Group,
76 Nelson St, Maryborough, Victoria 3465, Australia.
www.mcphersonsprinting.com.au

10 9 8 7 6 5 4 3 2 1

Contents

Not to Scale

Nim's Island

Wendy Orr

pictures by Kerry Millard

With thanks to my parents, who searched their log books and photograph albums to help build Nim's Island, and to all my family, friends and internet acquaintances who answered my requests for odd information on coconuts, whistling shells and broken rudders.

W.O.

1

IN A PALM TREE, on an island, in the middle of the wide blue sea, was a girl.

Nim's hair was wild, her eyes were bright, and around her neck she wore three cords. One was for a spyglass, one for a whirly, whistling shell and the other a fat, red pocket-knife in a sheath.

With the spyglass at her eye, she watched her father's boat. It sailed out through the reef to the deeper dark ocean, and Jack turned to wave and Nim waved back, though she knew he couldn't see.

Then the white sails caught the wind and blew him out of sight, and Nim was alone. For three days and three nights, whatever happened or needed doing, Nim would do it.

'And what we need first,' said Nim, 'is breakfast!' So she threw four ripe coconuts *thump!* into the sand, and climbed down after them.

Then she whistled her shell, two long, shrill notes that carried far out to the reef where the sea lions were fishing. Selkie popped her head above the water. She had a fish in her mouth, but she swallowed it fast and dived towards the beach.

And from a rock by the hut, Fred came scuttling. Fred was an iguana, spiky as a dragon, with a cheerful snub nose. He twined round Nim's feet in a prickly hug.

'Are you saying good morning,' Nim demanded, 'or just begging for breakfast?'

Fred stared at the coconuts. He was a very honest iguana.

Coconuts are tricky to open, but Nim was an expert. With a rock and a spike, she punched a hole and drank the juice; cracked the shell and pried out the flesh. Fred snatched his piece and gulped it down.

Marine iguanas don't eat coconut, but no one had ever told Fred.

Now Selkie was flopping up the beach to greet them, but: 'We'll come in too!' Nim shouted, and dived off the rocks.

Selkie twisted and shot up underneath, gliding Nim through the waves, thumping over, ducking under. Nim clung tight, till she was half sea lion and half girl, and all of her was part ocean.

Then Selkie and Fred went to sunbake on the rock and Nim went back to the hut. She poured a mug of water from her favourite blue bottle, brushed her teeth above a clump of grass that needed the spit, and started her chores. There were lots today, because she was doing some of Jack's as well as her own.

~

LONG AGO, when Nim was a baby, she'd had a mother as well as Jack. But one day, her mother had gone to investigate the contents of a blue whale's stomach. It was an interesting experiment that no one had done for thousands of years, and Jack said that it would have been all right, it should have been safe – until the Troppo Tourists came to make a film of it, shouting and racing their huge pink-and-purple boat around Nim's mother and the whale. When Jack told them to stop they made rude signs and bumped their boat against the whale's nose.

The whale panicked and dived, so deep that no one ever knew where or when he came back up again.

Nim's mother never came back up at all.

So Jack packed his baby into his boat and sailed round and round the world, just in case Nim's mother came back up out of the ocean somewhere else and didn't know where to find them. Then one day, when the baby had grown into a very little girl, he'd found this island.

It was the most beautiful island in the whole world. It had white shell beaches, pale-gold sand and tumbled black rocks where the spray threw rainbows into the sky. It had a fiery mountain with green rainforest on the high slopes and grasslands at the bottom. There was a pool of fresh water to drink, a waterfall to slide down and, in a hidden hollow where the grasslands met the white shell beach, there was –
'A place for a hut!'

And, around it all, so that only the smallest boats could weave their way through, was a maze of reef, curving from the black rocks on one side to the white cliffs on the other.

Jack sailed back to a city for the very last time. He filled up the boat with plants for a garden and supplies for science, and landed on the island to build a home for just him and his daughter, because he knew now that Nim's mother had stayed down at the bottom of the sea.

Like a mermaid, Nim thought.

He built a hut of driftwood logs and good strong branches, with a palm-thatched roof and a hard dirt floor. He put up a satellite dish, and a solar panel to charge the batteries for a torch, a mobile phone and a laptop computer.

He made sleeping mats stuffed with rustling palm fronds, a table and two stools, a desk, bookcases and shelves for his science stuff, coconut-shell bowls and sea-shell plates. He dug a vegetable garden in the rich soil at Fire Mountain's base and planted avocados, bananas, lettuce, oranges, pineapples, strawberries, sweet potatoes and tomatoes, and bamboo for making pipes and useful things.

Then he went on being a scientist, and when Nim got older, she helped him. They read what the barometer said, measured how much rain fell every day and how strong the winds were, how high the high tides reached and how low the low tides fell, and then they marked the measurements on a clean white chart with a dark-blue texta.

They studied the plants that grew on the island and the animals that lived there. They put blue bands on the birds' legs and wrote down the numbers so Jack could remember the birds' birthdays and who their mothers and fathers were. (Nim remembered anyway.)

Sometimes Jack wrote articles about the weather and the plants and animals, and emailed them to science magazines and universities, and sometimes people emailed him questions to answer. He would tell them about tropical storms and iguanas and seaweed, but he would never tell them where the island was, in case the Troppo Tourists ever found it, because Jack hated the Troppo Tourists worse than sea-snakes or scorpions. Only the supply ship – which came once a year to bring them books and paper, flour and yeast, nails and cloth and the other things they couldn't make themselves – knew where they lived. It was too big to weave its way through the reef, so Jack and Nim always sailed out to meet it, and the ship's captain never saw just how beautiful the island was.

And every day, no matter how excited Jack got about finding a new kind of sea-shell or butterfly, they looked after their garden; they watered it if it was dry, weeded the weeds and picked what was ripe. Jack built a three-sided shed for the tools, with a hook for the bananas and his big machete to cut them with. The machete was Nim's favourite tool.

When they'd looked after the garden and fished for dinner and checked the beaches for driftwood or bottles or anything else that might have floated in on the tide, Nim had school.

That was what they called it, but it wasn't inside and it wasn't at a desk. They sat on the beach in the dark to study

the stars, and climbed cliffs to see birds in their nests. Nim learned the language of dolphins, about the tiny crabs that float out to sea on their coconut homes, and how to watch the clouds and listen to the wind.

Sometimes for a whole day they talked in sea lion grunts or frigate bird squawks or plankton wiggles.

Jack loved plankton. Nim's favourites were the ones that shone bright in the sea at night, but Jack loved them

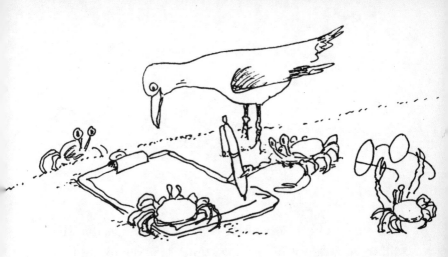

all, because they were so little, and so important because little fish ate them and bigger fish ate the little fish and the biggest fish ate the bigger fish, and there wouldn't have been any fish at all if it wasn't for plankton.

But Nim liked animals that you could see, and have fun with, so when Jack had said he was going sailing for three days to collect plankton, Nim had decided to stay home.

'I'll phone every night at sunset,' said Jack. 'And then you can check the email. If you don't hear from me or see me for three days, send an SOS.'

But Nim knew that Jack would be okay because he was the best sailor on the ocean, and Jack knew that Nim would be okay because Selkie was always with her, and Selkie sometimes forgot that Nim was strong and smart, and looked after her as if she was a tiny pup.

Even when the king of the sea lions barked at her to come and fish or snuggle down at night with her sea lion family, Selkie stayed close to Nim.

2

ALL THAT FIRST DAY alone Nim did the things that she did when Jack was home. Sometimes she even forgot that he wasn't just somewhere else on the island, measuring the bubbles at the Hissing Stones or counting eggs in a kittywake's nest.

But when she went to bed, the wind began to blow.

It had been the tiniest breeze as she sat on the beach to watch the sun go down and wait for the phone to ring; the barest stirring of the palms as Jack said hello.

'Did you find interesting plankton?' she asked.

'Millions,' said Jack. 'Trillions. And some greedy birds who thought I was fishing.'

'Far-away birds?'

'Home birds. The big one you call Galileo swooped me in case my microscope was a fish. I told him to go home and bother you.'

Nim laughed. 'He did! I only caught one fish all afternoon – and he snitched it right out of my hand! So I gave up and read on Selkie's Rock.'

'Good book?'

'*Mountain Madness.* You said it was your very favourite, remember?'

'So I did,' said Jack.

'Because it's exciting?'

'I liked the people in it,' said Jack. 'I felt as if the Hero could be my friend.'

'It'd be funny having a friend that could talk.'

'Honk, whuffle, grunt,' said Jack in his best sea lion voice. 'Selkie can talk! She's just not very good at telling stories.'

Nim patted Selkie in case that hurt her feelings.

'Don't forget to check the email,' Jack went on. 'Say I'll answer in a few days. Unless it's the Troppo Tourists – I'd rather meet six hungry sharks than that pink-and-purple boat!'

'I'd rather meet a cyclone at sea!'

'I'd rather jump in the fire from Fire Mountain ... or talk to Nim when she hasn't had enough sleep!' said Jack. 'Don't stay up too late reading!'

So Nim blew iguana kisses into the phone, and went back to the hut, and the breeze flicked her hair and was cool against her cheek.

It was already dark in the hut, and when she checked the email, even though she didn't know anyone in the wide, wide world who might send her a letter, it made her lonely to see 'No Messages' in the email box on the screen.

'Goodnight, Selkie!' Nim called. 'Goodnight, Fred!'

Fred was already asleep in his little rock cave beside the hut, but there was a quiet honk from Selkie's Rock.

Nim lay down on her mat with her torch and her book.

The waves rumbled onto the reef and mumbled across the sand. The breeze whistled through the cracks in the walls, and there was no comforting noise of Jack humming to himself or turning pages.

Nim felt excited and brave and a tiny bit afraid, but the second chapter of *Mountain Madness* was even more exciting than the first, and she thought about the Hero till she went to sleep.

The wind grew stronger. It howled at the door and screamed through the windows; it laughed at Nim because Jack wasn't there, and she didn't know if it was just teasing her or was going to grow to a tree-throwing, hut-smashing storm.

She switched on the torch and crept outside.

The clouds were scudding across the moon; the stars had disappeared and there was a lashing of rain. Nim stumbled and nearly dropped her torch, but she could see Selkie's shape, darker than the night, and heard her bark, deeper than the wind.

Selkie nuzzled Nim's shoulder and curled tight around her. The wind passed, the tail of a storm roaring out to sea, and Nim was snug in her sea lion shelter, breathing the warm smell of fur.

Next morning, coconuts were scattered over the beach and the hut had a dent in the roof, but the solar panel was safe and the satellite dish, sitting above the hut like a fat white coconut, was still waiting for messages to bounce across the world and into Jack's email.

Inside, the hut was gritty with sand. *Mountain Madness* had blown open, and a piece of newspaper Jack had used as a bookmark was stuck against a wall. Nim tucked it back inside the cover, and started cleaning the hut.

She shook her sleeping mat outside the door, swept out the sand, and used a scrap of old T-shirt to dust the laptop and Jack's science stuff, her polished driftwood, a threaded wreath of shells and the picture of her mother.

Her mother had bright, clever eyes and a wide, funny smile; she looked happy-excited because it was the morning she went diving to investigate the contents of the blue whale's stomach.

Nim put the photo back on the shelf.

She put her empty water bottles into her wagon and whistled for Fred – Fred liked going wherever Nim went, especially places where Selkie couldn't follow. He curled spikily around her neck and they towed the wagon across the grassland, up to the tangled vines and ferns of rainforest.

At the edge of the rainforest was a wide rock pool with a waterfall tumbling into it, and on the other side of the pool was the garden.

There were plants to prop up that had toppled over in the wind, weeds to pull and strawberries to nibble, and a huge bunch of bananas just green enough to pick.

Nim liked bananas, but what she liked even better was swinging Jack's machete. It was shiny and sharp and made her feel like a pirate.

'Aargh, me hearties!' she shouted, and chopped down the bunch.

She dragged them to the shed and hooked them to a rope looping over a beam in the roof.

'I'm swinging the bananas!' And she grabbed the rope just above her head. Fred jumped and clung to the end with his claws. Swinging hard and heavy, they hoisted the bananas up to the roof to ripen.

It would have been easier if Selkie had helped, but sea lions aren't much good at swinging on ropes.

Nim put the machete away. 'Are you hot?'

Fred knew what she was thinking. He raced her up the path to the top of the waterfall.

Over thousands of years, the water trickling down the mountain had worn away the steep black rocks to make a curving slide. It was perfect for *whooshing* a girl and an iguana over bumps and dips and splashing them into the pool at the bottom.

Nim and Fred ran up and slid down until it was time for lunch. Then Nim picked up a tomato and an avocado that had fallen off in the wind, and weeded quickly around the peas.

'They'll be ready tomorrow,' she told Fred.

But Fred didn't like peas, and he was getting bored. He started chewing leaves and spitting them out.

'I won't bring you up to the garden again!' Nim said sternly. Fred spat out the last bit of pea leaf and crawled into the wagon for a wild ride down the hill.

~

THAT NIGHT, when Nim sat on the rocks with the phone and watched the sun sink red into the waters, Jack didn't call. She pressed his number but his phone didn't ring and he didn't answer.

She checked the email and there was nothing there either.

Nightmare pictures sneaked into Nim's head: upside-down boats, sinking boats, boats sailing off into the distance with fallen-off people swimming behind…

She pushed the scenes away angrily. Jack was busy. He was concentrating on his plankton and didn't know what time it was – like when he was doing science things at home and forgot to eat.

She picked up her book, and soon she wasn't Nim any more, she was a strong brave Hero scrambling up a cliff, she was swinging across a chasm, reaching for the other side… and rubbing her aching eyes, looking up to see that the hut was dark and her torch beam was fading into the night. But she stayed being a Hero till she went to sleep, because tonight she liked it better than being Nim.

3

WHEN THE SUN rose pink over Fire Mountain, Nim phoned Jack again, but there was still no answer; no ring; nothing at all.

Nim checked the phone ... the satellite dish ... the connections between the solar panel and the phone's battery charger ...

But everything looked the way it should.

She checked her email, even though she knew he didn't have a computer on his boat.

From: aka@incognito.net
To: jack.rusoe@explorer.net
Date: Tuesday 30 March, 22:21

Dear Jack Rusoe

Your article 'The Life Cycle of the Coconut Palm' was as fascinating as a feature film and as fact-filled as a documentary! But I still have a couple of questions ...

1) How long do coconuts float?
2) Do they float well enough to make a raft?
3) How could I build one?

Thank you, Alex Rover

'A letter!' said Nim.

She knew it wasn't hers; she knew that Alex Rover was just asking Jack a science question – but it was still a letter. It was as if someone, somewhere in the world, knew she was alone and was saying hello.

```
From: jack.rusoe@explorer.net
To:    aka@incognito.net
Date: Wednesday 31 March, 6:45
```

Dear Alex Rover

Jack is busy doing science. I hope he will answer your questions tomorrow or maybe the day after.

From Nim

She had heaps to do, and that was good because she didn't want time to worry about Jack.

She made banana-and-coconut mush and snuggled warmly with Selkie to eat it for breakfast. Fred always forgot that he didn't like bananas, so he snitched a bit from her bowl and spat it out across the rock.

'Yuck, Fred!' said Nim. She didn't feel much like eating now, either.

She watered her garden with bamboo pipes trickling coolly from the pool. She towed wagonloads of seaweed to spread around the plants. She picked ten ripe strawberries and a handful of peas.

Jack loved strawberries.

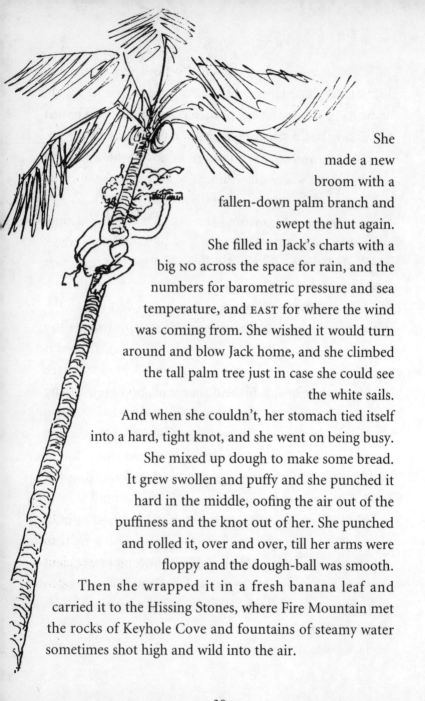

She
made a new
broom with a
fallen-down palm branch and
swept the hut again.
She filled in Jack's charts with a
big NO across the space for rain, and the
numbers for barometric pressure and sea
temperature, and EAST for where the wind
was coming from. She wished it would turn
around and blow Jack home, and she climbed
the tall palm tree just in case she could see
the white sails.
And when she couldn't, her stomach tied itself
into a hard, tight knot, and she went on being busy.
She mixed up dough to make some bread.
It grew swollen and puffy and she punched it
hard in the middle, oofing the air out of the
puffiness and the knot out of her. She punched
and rolled it, over and over, till her arms were
floppy and the dough-ball was smooth.
Then she wrapped it in a fresh banana leaf and
carried it to the Hissing Stones, where Fire Mountain met
the rocks of Keyhole Cove and fountains of steamy water
sometimes shot high and wild into the air.

Today there was just the small yellow pool splattering slimy bubbles, and the rocks around, too hot to touch, hissing steam from every crack. And the smell, like a rotten frigate bird's egg smashed on the beach.

Nim squatted at the edge, out of the way of the wind and stink. She shaped her dough into eight flat pancakes and flicked them one by one onto the hot rock.

What Nim liked best about cooking bread was watching the dough she'd mixed from dry flour, yeast and water puff into warm fresh bread. 'Science,' Jack said, but Nim thought it was magic.

Today it was nothing.

Today, when the bread bubbled and puffed in the middle, it didn't even make her smile. When she flipped it over with her bamboo flipping stick and then neatly back into her banana leaf, it was just bread, because cooking bread was what she had to do today. And if she did everything that she was supposed to, then Jack would come home tonight and everything would be all right.

So she went on doing jobs, busy busy busy all day. She heaped fallen branches into a bonfire; beach-combed from the Black Rocks of Keyhole Cove to Shell Beach in front of the hut, and then from the sands of Turtle Beach right to the Frigate Bird Cliffs at the end. (And she found three giant seeds shaped like hearts, ten new sea-shells and half a wooden paddle that made her think, Oh, no! But it wasn't Jack's.)

Suddenly she was too tired to do anything more. She made a banana sandwich and curled up on the rock between Selkie and Fred to read the last chapter of her book.

When she finished she felt happy and sad at the same time, because the ending was warm and smiley but she didn't want to say goodbye to the people in the book.

'I'll read it again!' Nim decided, and read the title out loud, as if she'd never seen it before: '*Mountain Madness*, by Alex Rover.'

'Alex Rover!' she shouted.

Fred fell off the rock and Selkie honked crossly at being woken from her nap. 'Sorry,' said Nim.

She opened the book again and unfolded the newspaper bookmark.

ALEX ROVER – AUTHOR OR HERO?

The most famous writer in the world has written a new book: Mountain Madness (*Papyrus Publishing, $15.95*).

Cliff-hanging adventure; romantic love story – read it and you'll think you're living it! You'll feel the cold rush of wind as you jump out of a plane; the sweat on your palms as you abseil down a cliff.

So is Alex Rover the author – or the Hero?

He couldn't describe these adventures if he hadn't lived them. But Alex Rover is not a typical macho action-man.

Anyone lucky enough to meet him will find a very special human being – a mountain climber who finds poetry on the peak; an explorer who sings the glories of the stars.

Unfortunately, meeting him is not easy to do. He refuses

to give interviews or photographs. Delia Defoe, his editor at
Papyrus Publishing, claims that she has never met him – or
even spoken to him on the phone!

'We correspond by email,' she says.

'We correspond by email,' Nim repeated. It sounded
important and funny. 'I correspond with Alex Rover by
email.'

'Selkie,' she said, 'Alex Rover's a Hero.'

'Fred,' she added, 'I *correspond* with a Hero.'

Selkie and Fred looked confused. They liked it when
Nim used words they knew, like *coconut* and *fish*, *swimming*
and *Keyhole Cove*.

But Nim was happy. If Alex Rover could survive all
those wonderful adventures, so could Jack. He'd be home
tomorrow, just like he said.

From: jack.rusoe@explorer.net
To: aka@incognito.net
Date: Wednesday 31 March, 18:27

Dear Alex Rover

Jack is still away but I hope he'll be home soon.
I'm glad you're a Hero because Mountain Madness is
the best book I've ever read. It's like real life except
more exciting and everyone is so brave. And because
it has a happy ending when the Hero and the lady find
each other and fall in love.

From Nim

From: aka@incognito.net
To: jack.rusoe@explorer.net
Date: Wednesday 31 March, 13:32

Dear Nim

Aren't time differences funny? When it's night-time where I live, the sun's coming up for you. You're living in my tomorrow!

The other funny thought is me being a Hero – I'm as un-Hero as anyone can be!

I can climb mountains if they're made out of paper, and swim rivers if they're in my bathtub (with lots of bubble bath) ...

I'm not even brave enough to talk to reporters. That's why they make up stories about me – one reporter even made up my name, and called me Alexander!!

Yours, Alex (Alexandra!) Rover

Nim had never heard the name Alexandra.

Alex Rover had never thought that anyone could be all alone on a tiny island in the middle of the ocean.

And so Nim went on thinking that Alex Rover was a man, and Alex went on thinking that Nim was a girl at home with her mother and maybe brothers and sisters, cousins and friends. And they both thought that they understood each other perfectly.

~

FAR, FAR OUT in the ocean, a sail-boat drifted. On its deck, a man lay sprawled like a boxer who'd lost a fight.

A frigate bird, his dark wings as wide as the man was tall, swooped curiously.

Jack opened his eyes. He was hot, thirsty and sore all over. When he scratched his beard, his hand came back rusty with dry blood.

He sat up and remembered.

He'd been sitting on the deck, watching the plankton glow on the night-time waves. Suddenly a storm had come roaring, and he'd pulled down the sails, but the wind didn't care. It threw the boat sideways and he'd reached for the satellite dish as it smashed to the deck.

Now there was a cut on his head and the satellite dish was gone. And if the satellite dish was gone, his phone wouldn't work, and he must go home to Nim.

Jack's head hurt and his legs wobbled, but he staggered to the tiller. He pushed the tiller and then he pulled it, but it swung loose and empty in his hand and he knew his rudder was broken. If his rudder was broken, then he couldn't steer.

And if he couldn't steer, his boat was just a big piece of driftwood.

4

AT KEYHOLE COVE, the reef met the rocks in a huge ring. On one side were the worn grey rocks where the sea lions sat, and on the other the harsh black rocks of the wild east coast.

Inside the ring, the water was calm and a light, clear blue. The sea shushed in and out through a hole in the reef, but only the biggest waves could break over the top.

It was a perfect place for swimming. You could float on your back because if you started to daydream you'd bump your head on the reef before you floated out to sea. When you rolled over you could watch seahorses and shells and the open jaws of the giant clams with polka-dot fish racing through them.

It was the perfect place to do a Coconut Experiment and find out how to make a raft for Alex Rover.

So early next morning, Nim loaded up her wagon with coconuts. Fred climbed on top and she towed them across the grasslands (because it was easier than towing a wagon across sand and rocks) to Keyhole Cove.

Selkie swam around to Sea Lion Point, and sat and barked for Nim to hurry up.

But Nim got another load and then another, till she

had twenty fat coconuts heaped on the rocks, and then she hurled them into the water one by one.

The coconuts bombed in and bobbed up. Selkie barked louder and louder. Fred got so excited he dived in with the last one.

Nim and Selkie jumped in too. There was still lots of room in the cove, even with twenty floating coconuts. Lots of room for Nim to float and somersault and stand on her hands, and for Fred to dash and dive and Selkie to *swish splash* the water through the Keyhole Rock.

When Selkie was bored with splashing she grabbed Fred by the tail. It was Selkie's favourite game, but she was so big and Fred was so little that it really wasn't fair. Fred's legs whirred; he paddled faster and faster, harder and harder – but he couldn't get anywhere.

'Leave him alone, Selkie!' Nim shouted, but it was hard not to laugh, and Fred sulked at the bottom of the cove when Selkie finally let him go.

~

JUST BEFORE SUNSET, Nim tried to phone Jack again – just in case he'd forgotten; just in case his phone had been broken and now it was fixed – but there was no answer.

It was two days since he'd phoned. If he didn't come home tomorrow she could send an SOS: *Go and Find Jack!* But Jack wouldn't want help and she didn't want to send it.

She walked up to the pool to fill her water bottle and pick more peas for dinner. He'll be home in the morning, she thought. Something will happen!

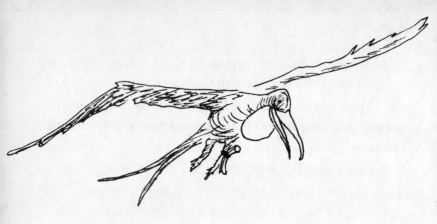

And something did.

A frigate bird dived to scoop a drink from the pool. Sticking out from his leg-band was a rolled-up piece of paper.

It was easy to call Galileo if you had a fish, but Nim didn't. 'Come here,' she coaxed. 'Come to me.'

The big bird teased and soared, turned and dived. He swooped over Nim, so low that his wings brushed her hair, and so slowly that she could pull the letter out of the band.

Dear Nim

I figure if I offer Galileo a fish he'll let me post this letter to you.

Had a fight with a freak storm. Storm won. Took my satellite dish, a bit of my rudder and a chunk of my forehead.

Can't figure out if I've slept for one day or two. Don't send an SOS – it'll take more than a broken rudder to stop me from getting home!

Love (as much as a frigate bird loves fish),
Jack

Nim ran all the way down the hill, waving the letter in one hand and the water bottle in the other. 'Jack's okay!' she sang, and swung Fred in a crazy jig around Selkie. 'He'll be home soon!'

Then she wrote two letters.

Dear Jack

I was SO HAPPY when Galileo gave me your letter. I didn't really think you'd forget to come home but I liked that better than some of the other ideas.

I've been very busy doing an Experiment but I'll tell you about it when you get home because I have to write an email now.

Love (as much as Fred loves coconut),
Nim

From: jack.rusoe@explorer.net
To: aka@incognito.net
Date: Thursday 1 April, 18:30

Dear Alex Rover

Today I started an Experiment to find out how you could build your raft.

I dropped twenty coconuts into Keyhole Cove to see how long they'll float. They won't escape unless there's a bad storm with really big waves.

I hope there won't be.

From Nim

She peeled a banana, dropped it onto a piece of bread and sprinkled it with fresh seaweed.

'1 message,' said the email box on the screen.

From: aka@incognito.net
To: jack.rusoe@explorer.net
Date: Thursday 1 April, 13:37

Dear Nim

My Hero would be devastated, annihilated, depressed and soggy if his raft didn't float!

What does Keyhole Cove look like?

I picture a ring of black rocks jutting out from the shore, stark against the blue sea – and bobbing ridiculously around in this idyllic pool, twenty coconuts waiting to be a raft.

The Coconuts of Keyhole Cove – sounds like a title! Hmm ...

With a thousand thanks, Alex

Nim read the letter three times. It made her feel warm and smiley, like finishing *Mountain Madness* – and when Alex Rover described Keyhole Cove, it was as if he knew the island, and Nim too.

5

NIM STOOD IN the doorway, looking out to sea one last time before the sun set, just in case Jack got home faster than he thought, because no matter how much she liked reading letters from Alex Rover, she'd like to see Jack's sails even more.

Through the shadows she could see, not a boat, but a browny-green dot floating in on the waves.

'Chica's coming!' Nim shouted, but Selkie and Fred had settled down for the night; Selkie grumble-barked but neither of them moved.

In a few minutes it would be completely dark. Nim pulled on her jumper and grabbed the torch.

Its light shone pale in the dusk as she jumped down the rocks to Turtle Beach. Walking slowly on the cold night sand, she turned off the torch and waited.

The turtle paddled steadily towards her, a hump of shell glooming dark in the grey waves, and heaved herself onto the sand.

Nim crept closer. 'Welcome home, Chica!'

Chica was too busy to answer. She dragged her huge

body up above the reach of the highest tide, and started scooping out sand with her strong front flippers. It was hard, grunting work.

Nim squatted beside her, watching quietly in the darkness and wiping away sand from the turtle's watery eyes, until the hole was just as deep and wide as it needed to be.

The stars scattered brightly and were mirrored in the sea; a fat crescent moon rose amongst them; and egg after round white egg rolled into the bottom of the nest.

'Ninety-nine!' Nim whispered as Chica pushed sand back into the hole, rocking her heavy body back and forth till the sand was thumped hard and smooth. She didn't want anyone else to know where her precious babies were hidden.

'Maybe in a few years,' Nim told her, 'ninety-nine turtles will come back and lay their eggs here too!'

For as long as she could remember, Chica had been the only turtle to swim out of the sea, back to this beach where she was hatched, to lay her own eggs.

'But maybe this year some of your daughters will be old enough.' She tickled Chica's wrinkly chin till her wise turtle eyes blinked with happiness. 'You can meet them when they come to lay their eggs – and then their daughters will come back, and then their daughters, and there'll be lots of turtles again!'

Chica blinked again, sleepily this time.

Nim kissed the top of her leathery head and followed the torch-light back to her own bed.

JACK DIDN'T KNOW why Chica liked to stay instead of leaving as soon as her eggs were laid, the way sea turtles were supposed to. Nim knew. Chica liked visiting her friends.

She showed it in the way she rubbed her throat across Fred's spiky back, let Selkie sniff her nose and Nim tickle her chin. She showed it in the way she nodded and blinked as Nim wondered about the places she'd been and what she'd seen, and told her what they'd been doing, and about Jack's broken rudder and Alex Rover's letters. Chica wasn't cuddly, but she was a good listener.

As the morning got hotter, they lazed in the calm shallows off Turtle Beach. Chica was tired because she'd swum hundreds of kilometres and laid ninety-nine eggs. Nim was tired because she'd stayed up so late watching Chica lay eggs. Selkie was tired because she'd worried about Nim staying up so late. Fred wasn't tired but he didn't mind being lazy if everyone else was.

Just before sunset Nim raced up to the vegetable garden to see what was ripe. She picked a lettuce and a tomato for a salad and dug up a sweet potato to bake in a celebration bonfire, with fresh limpets from the rocks and coconut for dessert.

From: jack.rusoe@explorer.net
To: aka@incognito.net
Date: Friday 2 April, 18:25

Dear Alex Rover

    I didn't check the Coconut Experiment today

because last night Chica came onto Turtle Beach to lay her eggs, and she likes me to sit with her while she does it. Chica is a green turtle, and she likes Selkie and Fred too, so we spent nearly the whole day with her.

Jack will be home soon too and he can check if I'm doing the Experiment the right way.

From Nim

P.S. Keyhole Cove is just like you described it!

From: aka@incognito.net
To: jack.rusoe@explorer.net
Date: Friday 2 April, 13:30

Dear Nim

I think the right way to do the Experiment is any way my Chief Experimenter wants to!

Now I'm imagining Turtle Beach: pale-gold sands marked by the flipper-prints of a very special turtle! And your footprints beside her prints ...

I'm turtle-green with envy!

Yours, Alex

ALEX ROVER SAT and stared at her computer. It wasn't easy to see, because the desk was stacked with books about oceans and islands, magazines about boats and rafts, videos about seabirds and animals.

The walls were covered by a map of the world, charts of the moon and stars; paintings of the sea: calm and blue, wild and grey, and every other mood between; pictures of sandy beaches, rocky cliffs, coconut trees, tropical islands, coral reefs, seagulls and frigate birds.

But Alex was thinking about Nim, and wondering whether Selkie and Fred were her sister and brother, or pets.

NIM WOKE UP thinking about Alex Rover's raft.

You can't hammer two coconuts together, she decided, but if I had a thin piece of board ... and lined the coconuts in rows ... I could hammer a nail through the board and into the coconuts.

But coconuts are hard to hold still while you hammer. They roll around so that sometimes you hit the wrong thing ... 'Ouch!' Nim yelled – so loud and so often that Fred went to sulk in his cave in case it was his fault.

After two hours she had a black-and-blue thumb and a pile of coconut for lunch. And one unsmashed coconut. 'Let's go and see Chica!' said Nim.

Chica was resting on the damp sand watching the tide go out. She blinked happily when she saw what her friends were carrying.

Chica's favourite game was coconut soccer.

That was what Nim called it, because soccer was the only ball game she'd seen a picture of – and because nobody else has ever thought of a name for a game with a girl, a sea lion, a turtle and an iguana all trying to be the first to get a floating coconut to shore. There were no rules except that

Selkie wasn't supposed to pull Fred's tail and Chica wasn't supposed to sit on the coconut underwater.

Selkie cheated a lot; Chica didn't cheat much but when she did she was very good at it.

So Nim threw the coconut into the water, and Fred dashed at it because he was the fastest and best at guessing where it would land, and Selkie sneaked under him and splashed the nut across the sea. Then she tried to throw Fred across the sea, too, but Nim saw her and shouted, and while Selkie was trying to look innocent, Chica grabbed the coconut.

She tucked it tight under her strong turtle chin and didn't even notice everyone tickling and pulling, wrestling and shoving. She towed them all towards the beach, and when she got to the edge of the water, she sank to the bottom with the coconut under her, and wouldn't move. And since no one could move Chica if she didn't want them to, that was the end of the game.

'It's a tie,' said Nim. 'Chica can't say she's won if the coconut's still in the water, so it's zero-all.'

Chica looked as smug as a green turtle can look, and didn't seem to mind at all.

~

LATE IN THE afternoon Nim walked around to Keyhole Cove to check the coconuts. All twenty were still bobbing cheerfully around the cove, bumping and floating, loose and free …

'I've got it!' Nim shouted.

From: jack.rusoe@explorer.net
To: aka@incognito.net
Date: Saturday 3 April, 18:20

Dear Alex Rover

I've been thinking about how you would make a raft.

Hammering coconuts onto a board doesn't work because the shell breaks, and if it didn't break right away I think bits of it would fall off later and then the raft might sink.

What if you put the coconuts in a sort of bag? How would you make the bag?

Where are you going on your raft?

From Nim

From: aka@incognito.net
To: jack.rusoe@explorer.net
Date: Saturday 3 April, 13:23

Dear Nim

I feel like a Queen Bee, lazing while you buzz!

A bag-raft sounds perfect. Now I just need a reason for Hero to find a large sack on a deserted tropical island! Or maybe the Bad Guys stick him in a sack when they throw him overboard! As long as they don't tie it up too well.

My Hero's going to a tiny Pacific Island, where, faster than a shopper at a half-price sale, he'll set off again to rescue the Lady Hero. (I'll be sitting at home, snug as a snail in its shell!)

I've attached a map I've drawn for the story – click on the paper-clip icon.

With best wishes, Alex

Nim clicked.

Her stomach somersaulted.

She stared at the map on the wall and the map on the screen and the map on the wall again.

Jack liked maps; he drew maps of their island, the currents around it and the places where they'd sailed. And because their island wasn't on the big map of the world, he'd drawn it on that too, near the crossing of two lines – the one going around the world's middle like a belt, and an up-and-down line curving with the shape of the earth.

'*This* is the Hero's island,' Nim whispered. And that must mean …

'Selkie! Fred!' she shouted. 'Alex Rover's been to our island!'

'I think,' she added, a little while later.

It took a long time to go to sleep that night.

NEXT MORNING Nim sang her way through the weeding, the digging and picking. She hummed as she measured and marked her charts, and she sang so loudly when she climbed Look-out Palm to check for sails that a seagull dropped his fish.

'That's what we'll do today!' said Nim, and slid down the tree.

She got her fishing rod and met Fred and Selkie at Turtle Beach. Chica was grazing the seaweed just where the water started to get deep. Selkie didn't like Nim to swim out deep, but she let her dive and visit for just a minute.

Fred stayed with Chica to see if she'd find an interesting sea-plant he'd never eaten before; Selkie chased Nim back and went out deeper to fish, and Nim climbed up the rocks where she'd left her rod.

The rod was bamboo, strong and springy. Jack had made it for her birthday and taught her to cast the line in a whistling arc – the best part of fishing, Nim thought.

That was why she hated getting a fish first go: it was like finishing a ball game after one catch. Seven tries this time and then a fish dancing silver on the end of her line. It was a good one to eat, the right size … 'Sorry, Fish,' said Nim, and killed it quickly. That was the part she didn't like.

Selkie did, though. No matter how far away or how deep she was swimming, she always knew the instant that Nim had caught something.

'Wait!' Nim ordered, but it was hard for Selkie to be patient when fish were being cleaned and she was waiting for the guts and bits that Nim didn't want.

When the fish was cleaned and Selkie had
stopped barking for more, Nim wrapped it in leaves and
built a bonfire on the beach.

She dragged some fallen-down branches and driftwood
into a pile, and used dried palm leaves for kindling.

When Nim and Jack had a fire at night they used
matches, but matches were precious because they came on
the supply ship, so in the daytime they used glass and the
sun's own fire.

She unscrewed the lens from her spyglass. She pointed
it so that the sun shone a bright beam on her kindling. A
brown patch grew and glowed, and a small flame sparkled
on the dry palm fronds, caught the small branches and
began to roar.

Then she dropped a sweet potato into the hot coals and
toasted her fish on a long stick.

After lunch they all lay on the edge of the beach. The
tide rippled over them, and when it started to float them
away they moved further up. Nim got a book and read with
her legs in the water and the rest of her on the sand.

And every few minutes she looked up to watch for sails
and wait for email time.

From: jack.rusoe@explorer.net
To:　　aka@incognito.net
Date: Sunday 4 April, 18:26

Dear Alex Rover

I have never been so excited in my WHOLE LIFE!
(At least not since Fred learned to climb on my
shoulders when I whistled.)

Are you really the Hero and have you been to our
island? Because your map is exactly like our map and
your Hero's island is exactly where our island is. Is
that how you knew what Keyhole Cove looked like, and
Turtle Beach?

Are you going to come back?

From Nim

From: aka@incognito.net
To:　　jack.rusoe@explorer.net
Date: Sunday 4 April, 13:29

Dear Nim

This is as crazy-wonderful as – well, I can't think
of anything as crazy-wonderful as an author making
up an island and then emailing someone who lives
there!

I'll tell you how it happened.

I made up a story about a brave Hero and beautiful

Lady Hero who sail around the world doing Good Things for Science. To make the story exciting, I made up some Bad Guys who stole the boat, kidnapped Lady Hero and threw Hero overboard. But because the story needs a happy ending, I made up an island for him to land on, where he could build a raft and sail after the Bad Guys to rescue Lady Hero.

So I looked on a map, and I made a dot where there was an ocean current to help drift him to the island, where the weather was warm enough for coconuts to grow, and where it seemed like a good place for a volcano to have grown into an island, long ago.

Will you be my Island Eyes, and tell me what you see? Because I haven't been there, Nim, and I'm not Hero enough to ever go.

All the best, Alex

7

From the top of Fire Mountain you could feel like a frigate bird, floating strong on the winds and seeing everywhere you wanted to see.

You could see the island's shores and beaches, and the grasslands and the cliffs and the rocks and the forest.

You could see far, far over the sea, every way that it rolled to the ends of the earth.

Early next morning, Nim whistled for Fred and hugged Selkie goodbye. 'I'll be careful,' she promised.

Then she checked that her spyglass was around her neck, to look for Jack; dropped a notebook and pencil in her pocket, to write things down for Alex; and packed two bananas, a piece of coconut, a pancake bread and her bamboo cup into her backpack for a picnic along the way.

And she set off to climb Fire Mountain.

She stopped at the pool to fill her cup and shoved its bamboo lid back on tight, then she climbed on up, past the top of the waterfall, following the creek through tangling vines and fly-munching flowers. The air steamed and sweat dribbled. 'Get down and walk, Fred!' said Nim.

But Fred liked being carried, and he sprayed a cool saltwater sneeze across her neck.

'Okay,' she said. 'But we'll stop for a rest.'

The creek was shallow and warm, but they flopped in, and it trickled over their hot bodies. Nim lay on her back and peeled a banana; Fred stared at the coconut.

'Later,' said Nim.

Fred tried to sulk but was too hot to bother.

They climbed higher and the ground was gravelly and black; the plants were grey spikes and the creek disappeared.

Then there were no plants at all; just bubbling steam and the rotten-egg smell of the Hissing Stones, but a hundred times stronger.

'Pee-uh!' Nim coughed, and Fred sneezed a pathetic spray.

Long, long ago, the top of Fire Mountain had been a round green peak. Then, one rumbling, earthshaking day, it had poured out its heart of boiling, rolling, melting lava, and the round green peak had been blown away.

Now the top of the mountain was a sharp grey point, with a great smoky crater yawning below.

Nim wanted to look down into the crater, but the cloud of steam was too thick to see through and too choking to breathe. And the longer she stood on the rocks, the hotter they got, so she had to hop on one foot and then on the other, and then she had to run out of the smoke and away from the heat to the very top of the mountain.

She sat down and Fred climbed off her shoulders and they both took a deep breath.

'Picnic?' asked Nim, and they shared the coconut and the water. Then Nim ate her bread and her other banana, and looked all around.

No matter which way or how far her spyglass stared, the ocean was empty. There were no white sails, or anything else that could be Jack's boat. Nothing but a frigate bird, winging steadily out to the western sea. Maybe he'll bring me another message, thought Nim.

But first she was going to be Alex's Island Eyes.

Far below her was the top of Frigate Bird Cliffs, then Turtle Beach's pale-gold sand, the grasslands and Shell Beach, the hut, on to Sea Lion Point and Keyhole Cove, and finally the grim black lava-rock that stretched all the way back to the far edge of Frigate Bird Cliffs. The island was built in layers, Nim thought: beach and rock; grassland and rainforest and, last of all, the rocky Fire Mountain cone.

She picked up her notebook and pencil – but before she could start to write, the ground began to tremble.

Then the earth roared and the mountain bellowed and an explosion of red covered the sky. A fountain of lava, red and bubbling, shot up from the middle of the crater. Red and gold stars, hot and boiling, sprayed over the mountain top.

It was like the wildest storm, when wind and rain crash and great surf waves thunder, except that the wind, the rain and the waves were all made of fire.

Fred was
a streak of grey
flying over grey rocks,
and Nim's legs followed
him, as she ran for her life
down the side of the hot gravel cone.

But the gravel was deep and
crumbly, and Nim's foot twisted – and
she rolled and skidded and tumbled down
the mountain. She picked herself up and went
on running; met Fred by the creek where they'd
had their first rest, and they splashed on through
and ran some more. Nim's breath came in jagged
chunks; she was so hot she thought flames might spurt
out of her head like her own miniature volcano.

And just when they couldn't run any further, they
splashed into the waterfall's cold water and *whooshed*
gently down to the pool.

They sat in it for one refreshing moment, and then ran
the rest of the way back to the hut.

Selkie was waiting anxiously on her rock. She barked
when she saw them, sniffed Nim all over, and whuffled
sadly when she found the cut on her knee.

It was a big, messy cut, with torn skin, deep gravel grooves and lots of blood. Nim must have done it when she tumbled down the mountain but was too scared to feel it.

It hurt now that she wasn't so scared.

Nim stretched out on the rock and let Selkie fuss. She stared up, and Fire Mountain was still shooting scarlet stars, a glow of red on the grey cone, but the lava hadn't followed them and they were safe at home.

But she hadn't seen Jack's sails, so he wouldn't be home tonight, which meant there was one more thing she had to do. She took her fishing rod back to the rocks, and when she caught a fish she dropped it in a bucket.

Because sometimes Galileo came when he was called, and sometimes he didn't, but he always came if he saw a fish.

Dear Jack

Today I climbed Fire Mountain to see if you were coming but you weren't.

I didn't do any science measurements or write anything down because the volcano erupted when we were at the top. If you think Fred can move fast for coconut, you should see how fast he can run away from an exploding volcano!

I think I can see Galileo now so I'll say goodbye.

Love (as much as Chica loves soccer),

Nim

A frigate bird came closer, and it was Galileo, so Nim danced the fish in the air and called his name. Galileo swooped low and stayed long enough for her to pull out the letter that was tucked into his band, and stick hers in instead.

'Thank you!' Nim called as the big bird soared up to his nest on the cliffs, and she unrolled Jack's letter.

Dear Nim

Worked out best way of fixing rudder is to drill hole through tip (not easy underwater!), pass a rope through hole, and steer with rope.

Have drilled hole but had to jump out before I could get rope through it. Sharks around here must have tasted the chunk I lost from my forehead in the storm – thought it was jaw-snapping yum! and want to chomp the rest.

Soon as they forget about me I'll get that rope through and be on my way home! But the storm blew me a long way, so it'll take a couple of days.

Love (as much as sails love wind),
Jack

Nim read the letter, and then she read it again. And even though Jack had tried to make it funny, she felt more lonely and miserable than she ever had before. Even writing a long, long email to tell Alex Rover all about Fire Mountain didn't make her feel better.

8

WHILE JACK WAS waiting for the sharks to disappear and hoping that he could fix his rudder and worrying about Nim, he saw a ship.

Jack danced a jig and sang a song because he wanted to get home even more than he didn't want to be rescued. His song didn't rhyme and it didn't have a tune, but it said:

'I'll be home soon!
I'll see Nim tomorrow!
The plankton can wait
And everything will be all right!'

The ship came closer.

It was a cruise ship. A pink-and-purple cruise ship.

It was the Troppo Tourists.

Jack stopped dancing and stopped singing, his face was pale and his stomach was sick, but Nim had been alone too long and he knew what he had to do.

In the cabin he found the flags he'd never used: one with blue-and-white checks and the other striped; when he put them up together they said *SOS: Come and Rescue Me!* to any sailor who saw them.

Then he waited. The longer he waited, the more he didn't want the Troppo Tourists to see the island; he didn't want to talk to them and didn't want them oh-ing and ah-ing and taking pictures of his home, but the longer he waited, the more he didn't want Nim to be alone.

The sad flags fluttered from the mast, and he went on waiting.

But the Troppo Tourists sailed out of sight.

~

EARLY NEXT AFTERNOON, when Nim was sitting in a palm tree to watch for Jack, the ship came to the island.

Just a speck in the distance, so Nim cheered and thought how she would run to the furthest point of Keyhole Cove, and blow her shell-whistle and shout:

'JACK NEEDS HELP! LOOK FOR A BOAT WITH A BROKEN RUDDER!'

Then, through the spyglass, she saw the colours and she knew that she could never ever call out to this ship. Because no matter how much she wanted Jack to be home now, what she wanted even more was for him to be happy, and he'd never be happy if the Troppo Tourists came to the island.

And even though they didn't know it was Jack's island, if they passed the blue waters of Keyhole Cove or the peaceful sands of Turtle Beach, they'd know it was the most beautiful island in the world. They'd come back with curious tourists, and fill up the island with holidays and noise.

'Oh, no they won't!' said Nim.

She raced to the hut and turned on the laptop.

From: jack.rusoe@explorer.net
To: aka@incognito.net
Date: Tuesday 6 April, 14:14

Dear Alex Rover

I hope it's okay to write so early but could you please tell me right away what your Hero would do if the Bad Guys were coming to his island and he wanted them to go away and not notice it.

From Nim

From: aka@incognito.net
To: jack.rusoe@explorer.net
Date: Tuesday 6 April, 9:17

Dear Nim

It's okay to write any time (and it doesn't even have to be about coconuts!) – unless your parents have another rule.

When my beautiful Lady Hero was escaping from Bad Guys in Sands at Sunset, she disguised herself in old clothes and grease, till she looked so ugly they didn't notice her. But a whole island is trickier!

Somehow the Hero would have to make the rocks seem more dangerous, the reef more terrifying, the pale sands bleak and lonely – make the whole island seem like a creepy, scary place.

This sounds like an exciting game!

Your friend, Alex

52

The ship was coming closer. Nim would have to work fast to disguise the island.

The sea lions were on their rocks, coughing, barking, honking, all the usual sea lion conversation, but Nim interrupted, shouting and waving her arms. Selkie swam after her, barking reproachfully.

The ship came closer still. It was slowing down – it had seen the island. 'Bad boat!' Nim screamed.

Selkie looked confused. The other sea lions stared.

'Shoo!' Nim shouted. 'Get off the rocks!'

Grumbling and grunting, they slid into the water. Nim dived in after them, but Selkie blocked her before she'd gone three strokes.

'I'll go back,' Nim pleaded, 'if you stop the boat.'

So when Nim was safely on the shore, Selkie headed the other sea lions out to the reef.

The ship stopped, and lowered a small boat down to the water.

Creeping low, out of sight of snooping binoculars, Nim jumped into the tidal pools and snatched up armfuls of the iguanas' favourite seaweed.

The small boat cast off with a snarl of its motor, and the king of the sea lions bellowed back.

If a boat found its way in through the maze of the reef, Shell Beach would be the first thing it would see.

Crawling across the pebbly rocks and sharp white shells, the blood flowing red from the cut on her knee, Nim threw handfuls of seaweed from one end of the beach to the other. Fred followed, nibbling as fast as she could put it down.

'You can have coconut,' she promised him, 'if you'll bring all your friends to the beach.'

Fred looked at her. 'As much coconut as you can eat,' Nim said.

With a sneeze of surprise, Fred scuttled away – from rock to rock, tidal pool to sea – until the beach was covered by spiny iguanas munching free seaweed. From the reef it would look like a beach of bumpy grey rocks.

And maybe they would turn around before they saw Turtle Beach.

Nim sneaked back to her Look-out Palm, shimmied to the top and clung high and still.

The boat had nearly reached the first gap in the reef. It

54

was close enough for Nim to see the people inside, wearing pink T-shirts and purple caps with a stuffed fish on top.

Suddenly the gap disappeared, in a swirling, thrashing sea lion storm. The boat idled on past, looking for another place to get through – but the sea lions followed. The king roared his roar and the others bellowed; the splashing sprayed higher and the boat rocked wildly, and was slowly, ferociously, pushed out to sea.

From her tree, Nim could see something else. Galileo was circling the boat.

Galileo had never seen pretend-fish before. Galileo's rule was that if it looked like a fish, it *was* a fish, and if someone else had that fish, Galileo would steal it.

He called to his mate, and they dived together to snatch two fish-caps from the heads in the boat.

The people screamed and swore, throwing their arms over their faces, but the giant birds only cared about the caps. They spat the first ones into the sea, and snatched two more to see if they tasted better.

Now the boat jolted, tipping hard as if it had hit a rock.

'Please don't get hurt!' Nim begged the sea lions.

The boat steadied. Its engine roared and shot it back across the water.

The tide was going out. By the time the little boat had been lifted onto the ship, the reef was jagged above the water.

So the Troppo Tourists cruised on past, but they didn't go away. They went as slow and as close as they dared, past Turtle Beach and round the point of Frigate Bird Cliffs.

Nim crept down to the beach and tried not to cry.

Chica lumbered up from the water, a smug look on her face and purple paint across her shell. Nim remembered the jolt. 'Did you hit them?' she asked, scratching under the turtle's chin.

Chica looked smugger.

Everyone tried but me, thought Nim. It stinks!

Turtle Beach stank too; stank worse than a bad day at the Hissing Stones. 'Yuck!' said Nim.

Half a dead shark had washed up in the tide.

'No one would land if they could smell that!' said Nim, and wondered if Alex Rover's Hero would use a rotten shark to fight for his island.

She sprinted to the hut and grabbed her wagon; dumped in the shark, slimy and rotting. It was a long, puffing haul to the Hissing Stones but Nim would have pulled it to the top of Fire Mountain if she'd had to.

The steam was drifting out to sea. It wasn't an extra-stinky day, but, 'I'll fix that!' said Nim.

She dragged the shark out of the wagon and across the biggest vent, where steam hissed out between the stones.

The steam stopped coming out, and the shark didn't smell any worse than it had before.

'What else stinks?' Nim wondered.

Sometimes seaweed washed up on the Black Rocks. If it didn't dry out and it didn't wash away, after a while it began to rot. Nim scrambled up and collected shirt-fulls of putrid sea-muck. She poked her head around the point. The ship was cruising past the breakers where the Black Rocks met the reef.

Nim clutched her seaweed and tumbled down boulders to the Hissing Stones. The shark smelled so bad now, she wanted to vomit, but she dumped the seaweed onto the steaming vents and ran back to hide, out of the stench and out of sight.

The ship rounded the point.

For a long, long moment nothing happened. Nim had dumped so much muck that no steaming stink could escape.

It was too late to do anything else.

The ship was across from Sea Lion Point, right in line with the Hissing Stones.

The shark exploded.

The rotting seaweed fountained.

The built-up steam sprayed bits of rotten shark, seaweed and Nim-didn't-know-what in a rushing geyser far into the air. The gentle breeze wafting out to sea turned into a grey, choking, sick-making fog.

The ship turned and steamed out of sight.

~

THAT EVENING NIM was so tired she couldn't eat. And she felt so cold and empty inside, and so hot and itchy outside, that she took her torch and towel and went up to the pool.

Nim loved the ocean because it was always there, wherever she looked and as far as she could see, but it was too huge and powerful to understand and too dangerous to trust. The pool was easy to love, because it was so small that she knew every rock in it, and so peaceful she could float peacefully as the sky got darker and the moon and stars came out, while the muck and muddling washed away.

9

TODAY MIGHT BE the day that Jack comes home, Nim thought, and the day to make Alex Rover's raft.

She jumped out of bed.

'Oh, no you don't!' her knee screamed, and she sat down again even faster. Her knee was puffy and hot, red with oozey blood and yellow with pus.

'Yuck!' said Nim, but she got up again.

Very slowly, she hobbled down to the rocks with a breakfast coconut. Fred had remembered her promise. 'You'll pop!' Nim exclaimed after the fifth piece of coconut, but Fred went on eating.

Washed up on the beach, just below Selkie's rock, were two purple caps with ridiculous fish on top. *'That's* an easier way to call Galileo!' said Nim, and picked them up.

Behind the caps was a big piece of driftwood, and under the driftwood was a torn piece of fishing net.

Nim and Jack hated fishing nets, but – 'The raft!' said Nim.

The net was torn too jagged to make one big bag, but she could cut four squares and make two smaller rafts instead.

The net cord was tough and slippery. After a few cuts Nim had to get her sharpening-stone, drawing her pocket-knife across it the way Jack had taught her, one side and then the other, faster and again till sparks flew and the blade was smooth and fine.

The sun said it was long past lunchtime when she finished cutting. Her knee hurt too much to go up to the vegetable garden, so she ate the last banana with some limpets and seaweed from Shell Beach, and drank the juice from a coconut, because there was no water left either.

Then, sitting in the shade of a palm tree, she knotted the squares down the sides and across the bottom. She flicked the net – knot and pull – and Fred peek-a-booed from side to side. Selkie grabbed the end of the net in her teeth and tugged.

It's not easy working on something when a sea lion is playing tug-of-war with the other end. It took a long time to finish the two bags, then a long, sore limp to Keyhole Cove.

Selkie and Fred jumped in to help fish out the coconuts, which would have been more helpful if they hadn't kept playing coconut soccer instead.

'Stop being STUPID!' Nim screamed.

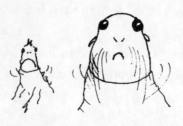

Fred sank to the bottom and hid behind a giant clam. Selkie humphed onto the reef with her back to Nim.

Nim, feeling smaller than the limpets she'd eaten for lunch, crawled up beside her. 'I'm sorry,' she whispered.

Selkie could never stay angry for long, but Fred could. Nim had to dive three times before she could coax him back up.

When she had all the coconuts on the rocks, Nim loaded ten into each bag and tied knots across the top so they couldn't escape. The sun was low over the sea by the time she dumped the second bag back into the cove and climbed on top.

The first three times she tried, the bag-raft ended up on top of her instead of the other way around. The fourth time Nim won.

She lay on her stomach and Fred rode on her back; she paddled once right around the cove, but she was in more of a floating mood today and the raft was good at that too.

But not with a sea lion on top. Selkie thumped onto the other one and sank straight to the bottom.

'Try both together!' said Nim, trying not to laugh.

Nim held the rafts and Selkie hauled herself on. She floated across the cove, nosing herself off the shore and bumping from reef to rocks. She liked it so much, she forgot to tease Fred; she could have played there all night, but:

'Sun's nearly set!' said Nim. 'email time.'

From: jack.rusoe@explorer.net
To: aka@incognito.net
Date: Wednesday 7 April, 18:25

Dear Alex Rover

This morning I found an old fishing net, so I made two rafts because I thought it would be easier than one big one. They are lots of fun to ride; Selkie liked them so much she barked till her throat was sore!

In Keyhole Cove I could ride sitting up but it's easier lying down, especially if your Hero was out at sea with big waves.

Fred and I rode together, and the raft floated so well we would have been dry if we hadn't got so wet getting on! Fred's not very heavy.

Selkie needed two rafts or she sank to the bottom. She's a bit heavier than Jack, so if your Hero is about that big he could float on a raft with twenty coconuts. If I'd known that, I would have made just one big raft after all, because Selkie sometimes slipped down the middle and I had to hold the rafts together for her to get on again. But I guess your Hero wouldn't bounce as much as Selkie!

From Nim

From: aka@incognito.net
To: jack.rusoe@explorer.net
Date: Wednesday 7 April, 13:29

Dear Nim

Robinson Crusoe couldn't have done better! I'll stop worrying about how my Hero could swim to the island if he was tied up in a sack. He can do exactly what you've done – though he'll find a piece of net just the right size for one big bag, so he won't have to fall down the middle like poor Selkie!

Here's the scene: he's gasping on the beach, realises that he's lying on a fishing net – and as he sits up, is nearly bonked on the head by a falling coconut. Phew! That was close! he thinks. Then – 'Ah, ha!' and he makes his raft, and paddles bravely out to sea to defeat the Bad Guys ...

Which reminds me – how did your game work out yesterday?

Yours, Alex

Alex waited, but Nim didn't answer. She'd turned the internet and laptop off, and was already asleep.

What kind of dog weighs more than a man? Alex wondered. Selkie must be huge! And Fred must be a dog, too; I can't imagine a cat riding a raft.

She stared out the window. From the forty-first floor, she could see a long way, but no matter how hard she tried she couldn't see Keyhole Cove or a Hero on a coconut raft.

And for just a moment, Alex wished that she could be a person who *did* things instead of writing them ... who could sail across seas or live happily on a tropical island.

But Alexandra Rover was a dreamer, not a doer. She was stuck in place like a train on a track, as much a part of the city as the Post Office steps.

~

IN THE MORNING Nim's knee was hotter and fatter, with red lines streaking around the ooze.

She didn't want to walk anywhere or do anything, but she had no water to drink and no food to eat, so Fred climbed on her shoulders and she pulled her wagon slowly up to the vegetable garden. She filled her bottles from the waterfall, cut off a bunch of bananas and picked some strawberries, and rode back down the hill.

Selkie huffed anxiously. 'I'll feel better after a swim,' Nim said.

So they swam around to Turtle Beach. Chica was grazing for seaweed, but she stopped to play a very lazy game of coconut soccer – though it was more like catch, because nobody could be bothered to wrestle for the nut.

The tide was going out, and when they'd finished the game Nim lay on her stomach and dug for clams with an old shell, while Selkie and Fred galumphed around the wet sand and Chica watched and nodded.

When she'd scooped out enough for dinner, Nim made a fire, baked her clams and split the coconut for dessert.

Fred darted his nose under her arm and nearly got bopped on the head with her coconut-breaking rock. 'Get out of the way, you greedy dragon!' she teased, and broke him off a piece.

Shining there, like a perfect surprise, was a round, creamy pearl.

Nim stared, not wanting to touch or move it. Jack had told her that sometimes, once in a lifetime or so, a coconut could make a pearl just the same way an oyster did, but Nim had never thought she'd see one.

Fred finished his own coconut – snapped – and the pearl disappeared.

And Nim felt as if everything good in her life had disappeared, too, and she knew it wasn't true and she knew it was silly, but she cried till her shirt was soggy and her breath was hiccupy and the tears didn't know how to stop.

Fred sat staring with his mouth full of coconut and pearl.

Selkie *whumped* him on the back with her flipper – and chunks of coconut and the pearl flew out of his mouth.

Nim gave one last hiccup and took the pearl back to the hut.

It was even more beautiful when it was clean; more wonderful than a shell's gleaming inside whirls, because it was whole and perfect. 'A Lucky Pearl,' Nim whispered, because anything so rare must be lucky, and to be beautiful and rare must be the luckiest of all.

She put it on a piece of stroked-smooth driftwood in front of her mother's picture and, since it was nearly sunset now anyway, turned on the laptop.

The light glowed, the computer hummed, but just as she clicked the email box open, the screen went black. She'd forgotten to charge the battery.

The pearl didn't seem so lucky when she couldn't tell Alex Rover about it.

THE NEXT MORNING the red lines and the yellow ooze, angrier and pussier than the day before, were back on Nim's knee. Her body was warm and her head was as fat and floaty as a cloud.

The solar panel was okay, the laptop battery was charging … the other charts and chores didn't seem to matter. She didn't feel like breakfast but Selkie fussed until she had a glass of water and a banana.

Galileo swooped past, chasing a booby bird with a fish in its beak.

Another letter was sticking out of his band.

'Thank you, Troppo Tourists!' said Nim, grabbing the paper as Galileo snatched the fish cap from her hand.

Dear Nim

Great news! Your fix-it father has got a fixed-up rudder – I'm on my way home!

Plankton celebrated too – put on a great show last night – AND I discovered a new species of Dinoflagellate *protozoan zoo-plankton!*

(It doesn't look EXACTLY like you but I named it after you anyway.)

Protozoan
Nim ←

The wind's against me, but if it doesn't get worse I'll be home tomorrow night or the day after.
Love (as much as big plankton love little plankton),
Jack

Nim knew she ought to be happy and ought to write a letter back, but her knee hurt too much to care and she needed advice faster than Galileo could bring it.

She dozed beside Selkie and, when she was too hot, went back to the hut. The battery was charged.

Just for a moment she wondered if Alex Rover still wanted to write to her now the rafts were finished, but there was no one else to ask.

From: jack.rusoe@explorer.net
To: aka@incognito.net
Date: Friday 9 April, 10:48

Dear Alex Rover

I'm sorry I couldn't write yesterday because I forgot to do the science stuff so the battery wasn't strong enough to turn on the email.

What would your Hero do if he cut his knee when he climbed Fire Mountain and now it has red lines and yellow gunk and his head feels hot and cloudy?

Also, does your Hero get lonely and miserable when he's on the island and the Lady Hero is with the Bad Guys? And even if he finds a coconut pearl, it doesn't seem as pretty because there's no one to share it with, because Selkie and Fred don't care about things like that (except when Fred tries to eat it, but that doesn't count).

From Nim

~

ALEX HAD WOKEN long before daylight with the story dancing in her mind like images from a film. She saw swaying palms and hot, gold sand, a shimmering waterfall and grumbling volcano, clear-blue sea and cloudless sky...

As the sun came up, she looked out at the dawn-grey roofs and railways – and put on the CD, *Sea Bird Songs and Dolphin Duets* – '*just like being by the sea*!' the blurb claimed.

'Not quite,' said Alex, turning on the computer.

She read Nim's email and she turned quite pale.

'It can't be true!' said Alex. 'A kid can't be all by herself on an island!' And she read it again.

Then she printed out all of Nim's other emails and read them again, and she looked at the map she'd drawn. She read Nim's email about climbing Fire Mountain and what the island looked like, and realised that Nim never ever mentioned another person.

'If one true thing has happened in my life,' said Alex, 'this is it.'

From: aka@incognito.net
To: jack.rusoe@explorer.net
Date: Friday 9 April, 5:55

Dear Nim

If my Hero's knee was very swollen and sore, he would soak it in the sea and then clean it up with fresh coconut juice and bandage it. Then he'd REST in the shade and drink LOTS of water.

And if he felt lonely and miserable he'd tell someone – maybe on an email.

That's what Girl Heroes on real islands should do, too.

Are you alone? Where are your parents?

Do you need help?

Love, Alex

Nim read the letter fast and turned off the computer. Her knee still hurt but it didn't seem as bad now she knew what to do. She took her blue water bottle down to the beach and sat in the shade of a rock with her leg in the water. Selkie sat on one side and worried, and Fred sat on the other side and slept, and Nim sipped her water and dreamed in the middle.

When she woke up
she was stiff and sore, and the
sun was going down. 'I've been
here all day!' said Nim, and she
didn't know if Alex Rover's
Hero would have sat there that
long, but she liked the way her
head felt as if it belonged to her again.

Then she took a clean hanky from the hut, and punched
a hole in a coconut and wiped the yellow pus and slimy
muck away from her knee, and now the knee was sore but
not hot and fat. And she turned on the laptop and read
Alex Rover's letter again.

'Oh!' said Nim, and felt pink and happy, because if Alex
Rover wanted to come and rescue her then he really must
be a Hero, just like the newspaper story said.

Even if she didn't need to be rescued.

From: jack.rusoe@explorer.net
To: aka@incognito.net
Date: Friday 9 April, 18:26

Dear Alex Rover

My mother went to investigate the contents of a
blue whale's stomach when I was a baby, but some bad
guys frightened the whale and she hasn't been seen
since.

Jack is studying plankton. He went away for three days except his rudder got broken in a storm and so did his satellite dish, but he sent me a message with Galileo the frigate bird to say he'll be home soon.

Soon might be tomorrow or the day after that.

I'm not alone because Fred and Selkie are here, and so is Chica.

So I don't really need help because I washed my knee like you said and it feels a lot better. And I'm happy that you're really your Hero, because I always knew you were.

From Nim

But when she turned off the laptop she didn't feel quite so bright and brave, so instead of going to bed they all went down to Turtle Beach and sat together till the full moon shone silver on the waves.

Chica would leave soon to wander the world's oceans for another year. 'But you'll come back next spring, won't you?' said Nim, because it was hard to think of Chica leaving too, when Jack wasn't home yet and Alex didn't need to rescue her.

Chica nodded sleepily.

'And maybe then,' Nim said, 'Alex will come and meet you, too.'

11

'IT'S A NIGHTMARE,' Alex groaned, keying in *Travel Agents* in the internet search engine. 'She's alone on the island and nobody knows about it except me. *Me!* – who's been afraid of aeroplanes and oceans since my uncle whirled me through the air and into a swimming pool!

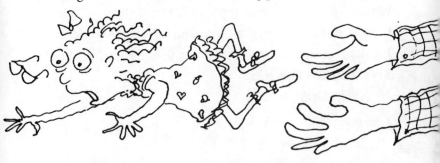

'I like being in my flat,' she moaned, clicking *Pacific Charter Flights,* 'with my books, my computer, and my imaginary friends. People who live in my head and go away when I put their story away. Places that fit into maps and pictures. Animals that don't smell or eat or leave hair on the carpet.'

'There's only one thing to do,' she said, clicking back to her email.

From: aka@incognito.net
To: jack.rusoe@explorer.net
Date: Friday 9 April, 13:52

Dear Nim

All my Heroes are just pretend. Real people aren't usually as brave – or as strong or smart or lucky – as the Heroes in my stories. Maybe that's why it's fun to make them up or read about them.

Because I'm not tall, dark and handsome; I'm certainly not brave – and I'm not a man.

But even if I'm not a Hero, and you don't need rescuing, I'd still love to come and see you, and the island – and, of course, Fred, Selkie and Chica. (What kind of dog is Selkie? I'm guessing that she's a Saint Bernard, if she weighs more than your father. And Fred's little – a poodle?)

Love, Alex

P.S. My phone number is 155 897 346. What's yours?

The letter waited, all the next day, till Nim checked her email again.

She stared at the screen. She read the letter out loud and the words stayed the same.

She turned the computer off and ripped out the plug, but the words danced in her head.

Alex Rover was not a Hero. Alex Rover was a woman, and she wasn't even brave.

Outside, the evening was peaceful and still, but inside

Nim was a rage hotter than Fire Mountain's lava and wilder than a whirlpool in a storm.

She felt angry and cheated, tricked and stupid, lost and lonely, sad and confused – and the feelings were stronger than the words could say. They jostled and shoved, spun, crowded and exploded.

Her shout rang across the water; birds settling for the night flapped into the sky, and the king roared an answer from Sea Lion Point.

Selkie, barking worriedly, lolloped across the sand. Fred peered from under his rock.

Nim was afraid that if she used the laptop she'd punch the keys right through the keyboard. She grabbed a piece of paper and a pencil and marched back outside.

To Alex Rover

It was horrible to trick me even if you didn't mean to, because whenever I was really lonely or scared or bored I thought about what you would do and then I could do it too. Which was stupid if you're not a Hero, and I wish I'd never done it and I especially wish that I'd never ever wished that you were my father instead of Jack.

I will never forgive you.

Goodbye for ever from Nim

Scrabbling in the dark, she found sticks and branches for a fire and when it was blazing, threw her letter on top so that the smoke would carry it far, far away to wherever

Alex Rover lived, and she would smell it and know just how angry Nim was.

Selkie and Fred crept up beside her. 'Alex Rover lied to me!' Nim told them, and threw another stick on the fire.

Selkie barked low in her chest.

'Well, not exactly lied,' Nim muttered, and rubbed tears on Selkie's warm fur, 'but she's not a Hero. I thought I knew who Alex Rover was ... he was my friend and now he's gone!'

Selkie grunted comfortingly.

'You won't change into something else, will you?' Nim asked, not sure whether she was joking or not. 'I won't wake up tomorrow and find out you're a mermaid?'

Selkie grunted again, a little louder.

'Alex thinks you're a Saint Bernard ... and she thinks Fred is a *poodle*! She must be crazy!'

Suddenly she began to giggle.

'She thought you were dogs and I thought she was a Hero!'

The giggle became a laugh, the laugh became a bellow, and she was rolling over and over on the sand, hiccuping and laughing, or crying, she didn't know which, until Fred sneezed and Selkie barked to make her stop whichever it was.

And she knew there was another reason that she'd sent the letter in a way that Alex couldn't read it.

So when the sun came up next morning, she turned on the laptop again.

From: jack.rusoe@explorer.net
To: aka@incognito.net
Date: Sunday 11 April, 6:45

Dear Alex Rover

Maybe you didn't try to trick me. I wanted to know someone brave because I'm not.

I think maybe I accidentally tricked you too. Selkie and Fred aren't dogs, but you will like them.

When are you coming?

From Nim

From: aka@incognito.net
To: jack.rusoe@explorer.net
Date: Sunday 11 April, 1:46

Dear Nim

Now.

Love, Alex

For two nights and two days Alex had been planning, sorting, packing.

Her time had switched to island time; she slept when it was night there and got up in the dark to turn on her computer at the island's dawn.

She'd refused to think about what she'd do if Nim said no. Because she didn't quite believe that Nim had stopped being lonely, and she didn't quite know if Jack would really be home soon.

And because nothing in her life had ever been this important.

She packed a first-aid kit, her laptop and mobile phone, two notebooks and two pens, *The Swiss Family Robinson* and *Robinson Crusoe,* a toothbrush, hairbrush and soap, two T-shirts, two pairs of shorts, one pair of jeans, one jumper, three sets of underwear and socks, and the map with the island marked with a dot.

Then she picked up her suitcase and locked the door behind her.

12

THE FIRST PLANE was a jet, big and solid, with nearly four hundred passengers and more crew than Alex could count.

'Alex Rover!' exclaimed the flight attendant. 'The world-famous adventure writer?'

'I guess so,' said Alex.

'Come and meet the pilot – he'll be so excited!'

'You,' Alex told herself, 'are a weak-kneed, spineless jellyfish.'

'Pardon?'

'I'd love to,' said Alex, and followed her into the cockpit.

'Alex Rover!' said the pilot, blushing red as a stop light. 'I always wondered – I mean … Would you like to fly the plane?'

'No thanks!'

'Not exciting enough for you?' and he showed her interesting things about the jet's instrument panel and engines.

All Alex could think about was what a very long way down the ground was; then the ground turned to ocean, and that didn't make her feel happier at all.

They landed after the sun had set, and when Alex found the little plane that would take her to the island nearest to Nim's, the pilot said they couldn't leave until morning.

'I can't land on that island in the dark,' he said. 'I'm not a daredevil like you!'

'I'm not a daredevil,' Alex wanted to say. 'I just need to get to Nim's island right away.'

In the hotel room the feeling was stronger. She felt like a tiger in a cage, trying to burst free.

Instead, she checked her email.

From: jack.rusoe@explorer.net
To: aka@incognito.net
Date: Sunday 11 April, 18:28

Dear Alex

I can't believe you're really coming! How will you get here and how long will it take?

I forgot to give you my phone number before. It's 022 446 579.

I've never talked to anyone before except Jack but I guess it works the same way.

From Nim

From: aka@incognito.net
To: jack.rusoe@explorer.net
Date: Sunday 11 April, 22:00

Dear Nim

Curses, curses! I can't go any farther tonight, and now it's too late to phone!

I'm flying to Sunshine Island at dawn, to meet
a boat from the adventure-cruise company Troppo
Tourists; they've been as friendly as a salesman with a
sick car to sell – and have offered to take me right to
your island, though I haven't told them yet where it is.

Nim, it's been so much fun writing to you – no matter
what happens, I'm glad I tried to come and meet you.

See you tomorrow!

Love, Alex

⁓

NIM WOKE UP when it was still dark, excited as Christmas.
She switched on the lamp and checked the email.

⁓

ALEX HIT THE alarm clock, and it went on ringing. She
reached for her phone.

'They're the Bad Guys!' a girl's voice shouted.

'Who?' said Alex. 'What?'

And then she realised. 'The Troppo Tourists?'

'They chased the whale when my mother died. Now
they want to bring people to stare at us and bother the
animals – and Jack hates them. You can't bring them here!'

'No,' said Alex. 'I think we need to fix them once and
for all.'

'How?'

'I've got four hours – I'll think of something.'

The strangest thing, Nim thought when she hung up,
was that it hadn't felt strange talking to Alex.

⁓

BY THE TIME the sun was properly up, Alex had showered, dressed, eaten a hotel breakfast and was waiting at the airport, but she still hadn't thought of how to get to Nim's island and keep it secret from the Troppo Tourists.

'Any daredevil plans?' the pilot joked as he started the engine. 'Going to parachute out halfway for your next book?'

'That's not a bad idea,' Alex muttered. 'I couldn't be more scared jumping out of a plane that staying in.'

The pilot went as pale as Alex's knuckles. 'But there's no land between here and where we're going!'

Alex studied the map and decided he was right: Nim's island was too far away for a detour in this little plane. Besides, she still had to meet the Troppo Tourists – the real bad guys, the reason that Nim didn't have a mother. If Alex didn't turn up, they might go on looking for Nim's island.

This time they might find it.

Alex's fear disappeared, as suddenly and completely as if it had fallen out of the plane without a parachute.

Instead she was angry. For the first time she knew exactly how her Hero felt when he was fighting the Bad Guys: 'And,' she muttered, 'I'm going to win!'

The pilot was still worried that she was going to jump out the window. 'We're nearly there,' he said. 'The airport's just past the sailing school – you can see the little boats now.'

Alex stared out and tried not to notice that her stomach

was diving faster than the plane. That's interesting, she thought. I can feel angry and sick at the same time!

'Do they give lessons?' she asked, because if she was talking she mightn't throw up.

'Give lessons, sell boats ... Is your next book about sailing?'

'Partly,' said Alex. She couldn't talk very well because a sneaky little fear had crept back and she was holding her breath to help the plane land.

~

TWO HOURS LATER she was wetter than she'd ever been and knew more than she'd ever wanted to about the way small sail-boats flip upside down and how it feels to be the person flipping off them. But she also knew how to get back on and push the boat right-side up, and how to pull the sails and steer.

And she was the owner of a small blue sail-boat.

'Not bad for a beginner,' the sailing-school owner said, pocketing her money. 'But don't go too far from the shore!'

Alex tried to smile.

'Funny,' the woman continued, 'you've got the same name as the adventure writer. But I don't reckon he'd need sailing lessons!'

'Neither do I, now!' Alex told herself. 'I'm ready to go!' And she tried to believe it.

She loaded her suitcase into the little boat and sailed out of the sailing-school cove, around the corner to the pink-and-purple Troppo Tourists ship.

'Ahoy there!' she shouted, jumping onto the wharf and standing up as tall and brave as she could.

The captain came running down the gangplank. '*You're* Alex Rover? But you're ... what a delightful surprise!'

'Are you going to write a book about us?' asked one of the crew.

'Maybe,' said Alex.

'We'll have to make a good impression,' the captain smiled, trying to suck his stomach in behind his Troppo T-shirt.

'I'm sure you will,' said Alex. 'Do you mind if I bring my little boat?'

'You there!' the captain shouted at two of the crew. 'Hoist this boat up on deck.'

'Now,' he went on, rubbing his hands excitedly, 'can you tell us where this island is?'

84

Alex pointed to a spot on the chart, a little way east of Nim's island.

'We'd love to hear more about it,' the captain said, and started the motor.

The crew gathered round as Alex began.

Alex was a storyteller. She spent her life telling stories on paper, and she made people laugh and cry and hold their breath, but she had never told a story as important as this.

She spoke quietly, and the crew huddled nearer, caught in the net of her words.

'Long, long ago, when the world was young, a volcano began to grow, deep under the sea. It grew slowly, day by day and year by year, pulling lava from the heart of the earth – rolling, boiling, melting rock, hotter than fire, hot as the sun.

'Then, one bright summer day – a day just like today, a day just like a million other bright summer days – the mountain under the sea *exploded.*'

She hissed the word out, her hands and eyes opening wide. The crew shivered.

'With a roar that shook the earth, a storm came: thunder crashed and lightning flashed; winds howled, and waves towered. From the heart of the volcano, melted rock and boiling lava poured up and out, higher and higher. And when it had finished and the boiling rock had cooled to stone, the tiny underwater mountain had grown to a full-grown island with its head poking out from the sea.

'Now, some islands,' Alex went on, as the Troppo

Tourists sat silent and still around her, 'become peaceful once they've been born from the sea. But this island didn't. This island stayed hot and angry.

'Its volcano still shoots fire; boiling lava still tumbles down its slopes and the stench of hell floats in its mists. Its rocks are black and sharp and its cliffs are steep.'

'No golden sand?' the captain asked hopefully.

'A little,' Alex admitted. 'But in front of the sands, curved from the rocks at one end to the cliffs at the other, is a maze of rocky reef – a treacherous, sword-sharp, boat-ripping reef.'

The crew shivered.

'Lions of the sea,' Alex continued, 'live on the rocks: the smartest sea lions you will ever meet, the fiercest and bravest in all the world, ready to fight to protect their home.

'And if a boat could pass the sea lions, and find its way through the sword-sharp maze, and not choke in the rotten-egg gas or fry in the boiling lava, when it reached the beach it would meet the dragons.'

'Dragons?' squeaked a crew member.

'Small dragons – but so many they could cover the sand, and, like the sea lions, they will fight bravely to save their island.'

She hurried on before anyone could ask how.

'There are birds, too, birds who are big and strong and tough enough to live on a mountain that shoots fire and choking gas. Birds who are so quick and agile that they can swoop down and snatch the hairs right out of a person's head.'

The captain twitched his hat nervously around his ears. 'Why do you want to go to such a terrible place?'

'It sounds even worse than that island last week,' one of the crew said. 'I'm not going there!'

'You don't need to,' Alex said. 'You're going to lower my little boat and I'll sail the rest of the way.'

'But why?' the captain repeated.

'To see if that's how my Hero escapes from the Bad Guys,' Alex lied, because she knew that if they saw the island, they might forget her story.

The captain giggled. 'That makes us sound like the bad guys!'

'It depends,' said Alex, and began the second part of her story, because it wasn't enough to make them frightened, and now she wanted to make them feel so bad that they would *never, ever* bother Nim and Jack again.

'My Hero is a sad, lonely man who once lived happily with a Lady Hero and their baby, helping the world with research and science. But one day, while the Lady Hero was deep under the sea studying a whale, a noisy boat came to spy on them. My Hero *begged* that noisy boat to go away, to be quiet, to stay away from the frightened whale – but they laughed, were louder, and chased that whale so that it swam right to the bottom of the sea – and the Lady Hero was never seen again.'

She whispered the last words. One of the crew sniffed, and one blew his nose and the others wiped their eyes.

'Are they bad guys?' Alex asked. 'You'll have to decide. Because that's not the end of the story.

'Now my Heroes live on this fiery, dangerous island, far away from good people and bad. But what if the noisy boat came back, with people to trample their lonely home; to fight their sea lion and dragon friends, and destroy the science they're giving the world?'

Tears dripped onto Troppo shirts; there were gulps and sobs and soggy noses. 'That would be a terrible ending!' said the crew. 'You can't end a story like that!' And they sobbed some more.

Alex looked at the captain.

The captain didn't care about Nim and Jack; but he was afraid of sea lions and dragons and boat-ripping reefs. And he was *very, very* afraid of being in Alex's book, because people wouldn't pay lots of money to go on Troppo Tourist tours if they knew the captain was a Bad Guy.

His eyes were sharp and cold as a shark's, but he tried to smile. 'A story should have a happy ending,' he said. 'Your Heroes can stay alone on their island, and the tourists can find somewhere else to explore.'

NIM SANG AS she did her chores. She didn't know how Alex would beat the Bad Guys, but she knew she would.

She did her charts and cleaned the hut; she dusted, shook and swept; got new palm fronds to make Alex's bed; arranged sea-shells around the coconut pearl and her mother's picture.

She weeded and watered the vegetable garden, ate two bananas and some peas for lunch; dug up three sweet potatoes and picked a lettuce, avocado, tomato and three handfuls of strawberries for later.

Then she flopped into the pool for a rest and a bath, and she and Fred watched the birds overhead.

They were flying inland, as if it was night.

Something was wrong.

Back at the beach, the sea lions were honking and restless, and Fred's friends were zipping over the rocks, even the oldest scuttling like hatchlings.

Selkie was by the hut, barking anxiously for Nim.

Two more gulls flew past, and then a frigate bird.

'Galileo!' Nim called, running to the hut for a Troppo Tourist cap. 'Have you got something for me?'

The big bird swooped, grabbed the stuffed fish and let Nim pull a note from his band.

Dear Nim

The birds say there's a storm coming.

GO TO THE EMERGENCY CAVE.

Take the phone, laptop, solar panel, battery charger and other scientific equipment, and whatever else you have time for – but you are the only thing that matters. As soon as you see that storm coming, drop everything and get to safety.

If I can beat the storm I'll be home tonight or early tomorrow.

Love (as much as a Jack loves a Nim),

Jack

Nim stared up at the sky. It was clear and blue, but the air was so still and heavy on her skin that she knew the birds were telling the truth, and she knew she had to do what Jack said. Nim didn't like the Emergency Cave, but it was better than storms.

And it was much better than being on a boat in a storm, and *much, much* better than being on a boat in a storm when you don't know the storm is coming.

'I've got to warn Alex!' said Nim, and dialled the number.

Alex answered on the second ring. 'I've learned to sail

and I'm on my way! I've just cast off from the Troppo Tourists' ship.'

'Get back on it,' Nim begged.

But a roar of engines drowned Alex's answer, and when the noise faded into the distance, Alex was saying, 'I can see a dot where your island is. I should get there quickly – the captain told me there'd be some wind soon.'

'It's not a wind,' Nim shouted. 'It's a storm!'

And then the satellite dish on the Troppo Tourist ship was too far away, and Alex's phone went dead.

Nim dropped her phone into the wagon. She tucked the coconut pearl into her pocket and pulled down the satellite dish and solar panel. She loaded the picture of her mother, the torch, battery charger, laptop and satellite dish into her wagon, and tied the solar panel on top.

Fred climbed on top of *that* and nearly tipped it all over.

'Walking's good for you!' Nim told him, lifting him down before he tipped it back the other way.

'Meet us at the Emergency Cave!' she called to Selkie. Chica would be safer on the sandy sea-bottom off Turtle Beach, but sea lions can't stay underwater forever. Besides, if she couldn't have Jack, Nim wanted Selkie in a storm.

At the Hissing Stones she had to leave the wagon and carry everything over the black boulders to the cave. The laptop was heavy and she was afraid of dropping it; the solar panel dragged and caught its corners in cracks in the rocks – but in four trips the whole load was safe in the cave.

'Now stay there!' she ordered Fred. Selkie had stopped to fish, but Nim blew the shell-whistle twice to tell her where they were.

The sea was still flat and calm; there wasn't a breath of wind. 'I bet I'm moving all this stuff for nothing!' Nim said crossly as she tugged the wagon back to the hut for the books and Jack's files of notes. They were heavy, and it took six trips to get them from the Stones to the cave.

'One more load!' she thought.

This time she grabbed her sleeping mat, water bottles, toothbrush, comb, clothes and barometer, throwing them into the wagon any old way because now she could see in the distance a whirl of dark air, black and yellow as a bruise, moving across the eastern sky.

It was coming fast; faster than Fred after coconut. Nim dropped the wagon handle and flew across the grassland. The wind hit just as she reached the Black Rocks.

It knocked her backwards and whipped her hair; it tore at her eyes and ripped the breath out of her lungs. Selkie grunted encouragement, Fred skittered, and Nim scrambled the rest of the way on her hands and knees. As she reached the mouth of the cave, the first thunder boomed and the rain came down like a surf wave on the rocks.

⁓

ALEX PULLED HER sails tight, the way the instructor had shown her. The Troppo Tourists ship disappeared; she was alone on a wide, empty ocean in a boat as small and frail as a bathtub toy …

I wish Nim was right and I was my Hero! she thought. But at least I can take notes about sailing – the gentle breeze, the interesting clouds …

The interesting clouds came closer, fast. They were dark grey and swirling. The gentle breeze jumped to a full-force gale, and Alex felt like the Hero in a legend who let the winds escape from the bag they were trapped in.

That was when she remembered that she'd left her life-jacket on the ship.

'I'll tie myself to the mast,' she said, but before she could reach it, the rain started.

'Like being in a carwash!' Alex thought. 'Without a car!'

The mast suddenly seemed a long way away, but just beside her was a metal ring with a rope through it. Alex yanked the rope free and tied one end to the ring and the other around her waist.

Then there was nothing to do except try to steer, and wonder whether the rope she'd pulled off was important, and did it matter anyway when the boat was balancing on skyscraper-high waves?

Maybe they weren't quite as tall as skyscrapers. Maybe they weren't much higher than a cottage. Tall enough! thought Alex as she roller-coasted from one to the next.

A fork of lightning exploded into a wave; a crash of thunder hit her ears like a boxer's punch.

Alex threw herself onto her stomach and clung to the tiller. Then the next wave was under her and the wind was howling and hurtling her towards the smudge of Nim's island – 'Faster than a city train!' Alex guessed.

She couldn't decide whether that was a good thing or not, but she was beginning to understand how her Hero felt when she sent him adventuring: terrified-thrilled; sure he was going to die and so alive that he never wanted to stop.

CRACK!

Her sails billowed like a balloon; the mast lifted and toppled off the boat. There was a sad flap of white and her mast and sails sank out of sight.

'So now it's a rowboat,' Alex decided.

She pretended that she was her Hero, because he wouldn't mind that his computer and suitcase had washed overboard and were at the bottom of the ocean.

He wouldn't even be scared when he saw that the

mast had taken a chunk out of the bottom of the boat as a going-away present, and the sea was coming in to take its place. A Hero would simply take off his hat and bail, so that's what Alex did.

The problem was that even when she was being a Hero, the waves were still monstrous, the rain was still pouring and the wind was still roaring, and each time they slammed across a wave, more of the wave came into the boat, and no matter how fast she bailed, less of it went out. The hole was getting bigger, and the bigger it got, the faster the water poured in, and the faster the water poured in, the bigger the hole got.

And the bigger the hole got, the faster the boat sank, as if it was tired of being a boat and wanted to try being a submarine.

And Alex was still tied firmly to it.

'If only I'd gone to Brownies,' she muttered, frantically trying to untie the pulled-tight rope, 'and learned to tie reef knots, or whatever kind of knot it is that you can untie when you need to!'

She tried to undo the knot around her waist first, but when she'd pulled it so tight that she could hardly breathe, she gave up and worked on the other end. She tried with fingers and tried with teeth, spluttering and choking, because now the knot was quite a long way under water.

Which is where I'm going to be, too, Alex thought, and even though she didn't much like being in the top bit of the ocean, she thought she'd like the bottom even less.

NIM LAY ON the floor of the cave with Fred under one arm and Selkie sheltering her back. Through the opening they could see the rain trickle to a stop and the gale gentle to a wind.

They crept out to look, peering out over the Black Rocks.

The sea was still monstrous. The wind had whipped it to a fury, and it wasn't ready to calm down just because the storm had passed. Towering waves crashed onto the shore; spray foamed white and rainbows fountained into the clearing sky.

It could have been beautiful, if Nim hadn't known that Jack was on the west side of the island, being tossed even farther from home, and Alex was on the east being thrown towards it.

'She'll be smashed on the rocks!' Nim cried.

She searched the horizon with her spyglass. There was no sign of a sail, but there was a speck that could be a boat with someone inside it.

Nim was still scared, but there wasn't enough time to

think. She crawled back into the cave and tore a sheet from her notebook.

Dear Jack,
  I've gone to rescue Alex Rover.
  Love, Nim

Selkie was waiting; Fred was starting to slide down to the sea.

'Wait!' Nim shouted. 'You can't swim out there by yourself!'

But Fred wasn't by himself. Chica had heard Nim's whistle, a storm-while ago, and had been resting on the seabed as close as she could get to her friends in the cave. Fred scrambled onto her back and hooked his claws to the edge of her shell, staring out over her head.

Nim hugged hard around Selkie's neck and they slid into the water.

It was hard swimming, even for a brave and determined lion of the sea. The waves slammed against them, so hard and so high that sometimes they threw Selkie backwards and under the water – which is where sea lions like to swim, but not when they're carrying girls on their backs.

Nim's hair whipped like long, wet ropes, and she gulped salt water with every breath, but she clung as tight as she ever could.

The seventh wave came; a swamping, dumping wave, stronger than Selkie, forcing her down deep below the water; stronger than Nim, ripping her arms away from Selkie's neck and pushing her deeper still, so there was nothing but swirling blue and she didn't know which way was up to the air and which was down to the bottom.

She was whirling ... struggling ... sinking ... but Selkie somersaulted backwards and pushed her up through the water till she was spluttering ... coughing ... breathing again.

Then the waves weren't quite so wild; they could ride up them and slide down without going deep under the water. When they were in the valleys they couldn't see anything but blue, but when they were on the top they could look around. They saw Chica and Fred, but never Alex.

They went on looking. Looking and looking. On and on.

Now Selkie was too tired to leap across the waves and pretend it was fun, but when Nim tried to be helpful and swim, Selkie honked a cross 'NO!', so Nim stayed on. She didn't know if she could have swum in those waves anyway.

She started to worry about what she was going to do if she didn't find Alex.

She started to worry about how big the waves were where Jack was, and how far away they were taking him.

She started to worry about Chica and Fred.

She started to worry about how she'd know when it was time to turn back – and that was the hardest thought of all, because it was the only one she could do something about.

She was worrying so hard that she nearly fell off when Selkie barked again.

Then Selkie didn't seem tired and Nim didn't feel worried; she blew her whistle as hard as she could and they charged across the waves to the small sinking boat.

THE WATER WAS up to Alex's waist, then her chest, and up to her neck; she was spluttering and ducking, and still struggling with the knots under the water.

She tried to think what a Hero would do now, but all she could think was that a Hero would have known how to untie the knot, and that was no help to her at all. She took a deep breath and wondered if it was the last air she'd taste.

A whistle shrilled – and there was the strangest, most wonderful thing she'd ever seen: a wild-haired girl blowing a shell and riding a sea lion across the waves.

'Ni—' Alex shouted, and then her mouth was under water, too.

Nim remembered the scene in *Mountain Madness* where the Hero was snagged by the rope around his waist as he climbed down a cliff. She grabbed her knife from its pouch and, as Selkie ducked under the water, Nim cut the rope.

Alex bobbed straight up to the surface.

'Nim Rusoe, I presume?'

The boat gurgled rudely and sank.

They looked at each other and started to giggle, choking with laughter and seawater and Selkie had to bark twice to remind them that treading water with one arm and holding onto a sea lion with the other, in the middle of a stormy ocean, is not the time to giggle. But when Alex heard Selkie bark, she said, 'So you're not a Saint Bernard! But you are a saviour!' and they laughed a bit more.

And then they turned back towards the island.

It should have been easier now they were going the same way as the waves, except that the waves were smashing onto the Black Rocks and they didn't want to do that, so they decided to curve around the reef and come in on the gentle slopes of Shell Beach. And Selkie couldn't carry them both.

'We could take turns swimming and riding,' said Nim.

But even going with the waves, Nim couldn't swim as fast as Selkie, so Selkie kept having to turn around, and Alex wasn't very good at riding, so she fell off every time Selkie turned around.

'I wish I'd gone to swimming lessons instead of writing stories about fish!' Alex muttered, and Nim started worrying again. She was getting tired, too, and so the next time Selkie circled back and Alex fell off, they both hung on to Selkie with one arm and swam with the other – but the island didn't seem to be getting much closer.

Suddenly there was a tickle under Nim's arm, and a sweet spiny head with a grinning dragon face.

'Fred!' she cried – and Alex, who had never seen anything quite as ugly and wonderful as a marine iguana, said, 'I'm sorry I called you a poodle.'

Following Fred was something that looked like a big bag with something else behind it – and *that* something began to look like a smug green turtle.

Chica had found one of the coconut rafts.

She moved steadily towards them, pushing the raft, disappearing as each wave rolled over her and popping up when it cleared.

Nothing ever upset Chica.

Selkie kept pushing Alex and Nim towards the island; Chica kept coming closer … and finally they met. Alex slid across from Selkie and climbed onto the coconut raft. She lay down and kicked her legs, but kicking Chica in the head didn't seem a good way to thank her, so she crouched forward and paddled with her hands. It didn't make the raft go much faster, but Alex felt better doing something.

Nim got back onto Selkie and Fred climbed onto her shoulders.

A few minutes later they tumbled onto Shell Beach, below where the hut used to be.

15

THE HUT WAS GONE, and Nim was too tired to start looking for what was left of it.

The last of the storm clouds disappeared from the sky; the sun sank gold and low, and Nim and Alex were still lying on the beach talking.

Selkie slipped back into the water to fish for her supper. Fred found some seaweed left on the beach by angry waves.

Chica gave them a long look and dragged herself towards the water.

Nim hugged her, as tight as you can hug a large green turtle. 'Goodbye till next year!'

'Thank you for rescuing me,' Alex said, and kissed the top of Chica's wrinkled head. Chica looked up at her and blinked.

It was always hard to tell what Chica was thinking.

'We need to go to the Emergency Cave before the sun goes down,' Nim said. She had a feeling Alex mightn't be very good at rock-climbing in the dark. 'We can have an Emergency Can for dinner.'

'And a coconut from the raft!'

'I wonder where the other raft went,' said Nim, but she was wondering even more where Jack was.

～

THE OTHER RAFT had been tossed out of Keyhole Cove when the sea went crazy, but it had bounced clear of the swirling reef waters and been caught by the monster waves raging out to the west.

And grabbed by an exhausted man with a scar on his forehead and a two-week-old beard.

～

ALEX WASN'T ANY better at rock-climbing than Nim had thought she'd be, but she loved the cave. 'Like Ali Baba's!' she exclaimed.

'I cleaned the hut so nicely!' Nim said gloomily. 'I even made you a new sleeping mat!'

Alex hugged her, and it wasn't quite the same as hugging Jack and not quite the same as snuggling in to Selkie, but it made her believe that the world might get better again.

～

NIM WOKE TO see Alex sitting at the door of the cave, watching the sun rise over Fire Mountain. 'And look at the sea!' said Alex.

The waves rolled gently, washed-clean and blue. Birds soared and swooped, screeched and fished; iguanas and lizards scrabbled; sea lions lazed and their king's *honk!* echoed across the water.

Selkie whuffled good morning. But when Nim had

hugged her and rubbed noses, Selkie slid down the rocks, and a moment later her brown head popped up at Sea Lion Point, beside the king's.

Fred grazed for seaweed in the tidal pools. He didn't quite trust this ocean yet.

Nim and Alex had a coconut and Emergency Rice Pudding for breakfast, set up the satellite dish and the solar panel on a flat rock above the cave; plugged the torch, computer and phone in to charge, and went out to explore.

They went to Turtle Beach, Sea Lion Point, the Hissing Stones and Keyhole Cove – 'Where it all began!' said Alex.

'Because if I hadn't done the experiment ... '

' ... I wouldn't have been able to write back again ... '

' ... and you would never have come!'

Already that seemed impossible.

They went on exploring. Nim's beautiful island was shredded and messy with bits of hut, pieces of shirts and desk, coconuts, palm branches, broken trees and lying-down bushes.

'As if a giant had a tantrum!' Alex exclaimed.

The garden was worse. It looked as if Selkie had taken her sea lion family up for a party. Pea plants were mashed, avocados were mushed and tomatoes were soup. Some plants had so few leaves it was hard to remember what they used to be.

The garden shed, with the bananas still on their hook, had been lifted right over the wall and dropped neatly in the middle of the bamboo grove.

Nim and Alex collected three green pineapples, a few mashed strawberries and scattered pea-pods. They hauled broken bits out of the pool and into the compost heap, and saved two avocados, a tomato and ten more strawberries.

'And the sweet potatoes will be safe,' Nim said, 'when we feel like digging them.'

They chucked broken plants off the garden and propped up the living ones, and when they were worn out Nim taught Alex how to slide down the waterfall into the pool, and then Alex told her stories till they were ready to work again.

She told her more stories that night while they tried to sleep on the hard cave floor.

The stories were funny and made Nim laugh; exciting, so she had to hold her breath; and something else that made her feel soft and warm and happy-sad, so she wanted to hug Selkie, except that Selkie had decided it was too hard to go all the way up to the cave for the night and was sleeping with the sea lions.

The next day they started clearing the grasslands and beaches, dragging branches into piles for bonfires, and coconuts into heaps for eating, and sorting out anything else that might have come from the hut or could be useful to build a new one.

And all the time that they heaved and carried and sorted, Nim worried about when Jack would get home and when Alex would leave. She hated the stories Alex told about her home in the city, because she wanted to pretend that Alex could stay on the island for ever and ever.

They took a different path to the garden and found Nim's favourite blue glass bottle, her comb, a good piece of rope under a dead jellyfish, and her wagon, hooked on a branch at the top of a tree.

The tree wasn't hard to climb, but it was a long stretch from the last safe branch, and when the wagon tumbled to the ground, so did Nim.

The scab rubbed off her knee, and it began to bleed again. Nim didn't cry, but Alex did.

'I had bandages, cream … a whole first-aid box for you!' she sobbed.

But she helped Nim clean the sand out with fresh coconut juice, and then Fred hinted that they ought to eat the coconut now they'd opened it, so they had it for lunch with bananas. And since they were at the pool and had a comb, they washed their hair and combed out two days of tangles, which hurt more than the skinned knee.

Alex looked so pretty, tugging the knots out of her long gold hair, and she was still so sad about Nim's knee. 'Wait here!' Nim ordered, and ran all the way to the cave and back again without even stopping to look out to sea.

'Close your eyes!' she said, and dropped the coconut pearl into Alex's hands. 'I was going to give it to you if you went away, but it seems like you need it now.'

'Oh, Nim!' said Alex. 'I can't take this!'

'I had it in front of my mother's picture,' Nim said. 'But a picture can't really see, so I want you to have it.'

Alex got soggy again.

'If I could have a daughter,' she said when she could talk, 'I'd want her to be exactly like you.'

Suddenly, the honking from the sea lions was too loud to hear anything else. Nim flew down the hill as Selkie led the whole herd into the water, splashing and barking at the strange shape drifting in through the reef.

And Jack staggered off the bag of coconuts and waded onto the sand.

Then he and Nim did a wild 'What happened? You're okay?' laughing, hugging dance, but Jack went pale as he stared at where the hut used to be.

'The science stuff is safe,' Nim said, but her father didn't seem to care as much she'd thought he would.

'I'm never leaving you alone a—' and then he stopped, and couldn't say anything more.

Alex was coming down the hill.

'There's something I've got to tell you,' said Nim.

16

ALEX KNEW IT was unfair, but she hated Jack. She knew he hadn't meant to leave Nim alone for so long – but he had. She knew he hadn't wanted Nim to be lonely, worried and frightened – but she had been.

She'd lain awake for an hour the night before, thinking of all the things she was going to say when she met him.

Then this lonely, exhausted man staggered in, looking beaten as a Jack Russell who'd picked a fight with a Rottweiler. He sat and stared at his daughter, and Alex knew there was nothing she could say that was half as nasty as what he was saying to himself.

And when some of the shock had gone from his face, he looked too much like Nim for Alex to hate him.

'Who?' he said finally. 'And how?'

'It's a long story,' said Nim. 'Tell us yours first: did the storm hit you?'

'Not the way it hit the island,' Jack said, staring at the tumbles of shattered trees, 'but fast enough that I hadn't put my life-jacket and lifeline on yet, and strong enough to blow me overboard. The boat raced ahead; there was no land in sight … but floating in the current just ahead of me was a raft made of coconuts! What's so funny?'

Nim and Alex couldn't answer. They were laughing so hard that they fell over and rolled around on the ground like sea lion pups. 'That's Alex's story!' Nim finally choked, and then they started from the beginning.

~

ALL THE NEXT WEEK, the three of them worked together: cleaning up the island, fishing and digging clams, collecting coconuts and saving the garden. Every night they built a bonfire with the broken branches they'd cleaned up during the day, and Alex told them stories.

Nim listened hard so that she could remember the stories forever, after Alex left, and tried not to think about when that would happen.

But it wasn't Alex who talked first about leaving.

'When are we going to build a new hut?' Nim asked one morning, when the island was starting to look like her home again, just with not so many trees.

'Maybe we shouldn't,' Jack said. 'It's time I stopped being so selfish. Maybe we should go back to civilisation so you can have a normal life.'

'This *is* my normal life!' Nim shouted. 'It's the one I want!'

She ran down the hill to Selkie, who left the king and snuggled comfortingly around her. Fred curled across her shoulders.

Alex and Jack went for a walk in the other direction, around the point to Turtle Beach.

'They're talking about what's going to happen,' Nim told her friends. 'But if Jack makes me leave the island, I'll run away and live here with you like I did before!

'Jack only wants to go because he thinks that's what a good father should do, but I don't want a good father – I just want Jack, and I know he wants to stay on the island as much as I do!'

She wasn't even going to wish the other part because it was too much to hope for.

The morning changed to noon; the rock got hot; Selkie, Nim and Fred went for a swim, climbed out to dry and went for a quicker swim; and still Alex and Jack hadn't come back. Nim was hungry but the knots in her stomach were too tight for food.

The king barked for Selkie. Selkie looked miserable, and then she looked confused.

'You can go,' Nim said. 'I'm okay.'

Selkie snuggled beside her a moment longer, but when the king barked again, she slid off the rock and into the sea.

Fred scuttled off to find some seaweed.

Alex and Jack came around the point and waded in the shallow water across to Nim.

They were smiling.

From: jack.rusoe@explorer.net
To: delia.defoe@papyrus.publishing.com
Date: Wednesday 21 April, 15:00
Subject: Really, this is Alex Rover

Dear Delia

I have a small favour to ask you.

All right, it's small like a giant squid, and you might think it's about as easy to handle, but when I tell you the whole story and why I'm writing it on a borrowed internet address (on a borrowed computer, wearing my new banana-leaf dress), you'll not only understand why I need a favour, you'll have a brand-new book. I promise you'll love it.

So ... could you please go to my flat and pack up all my clothes, books, papers and anything else you think would be useful on a small tropical island?

I'm attaching a shopping list. You'll need to find a good gardening and hardware store and a marine or boat suppliers as well as a department and grocery store.

The second attachment is a map. Please send the parcels by supply ship, parachute-drop or helicopter, whichever works out best. You can take the cost out of the huge amount of money you'll want to pay me for this next book.

Yours, Alex

Wendy Orr
Nim at Sea

pictures by
Kerry Millard

For Paula, who believed in Nim W.O.

For Wendy, and all of the stories we've shared K.M.

LONG AGO, when Nim was a baby, she'd had both a mother and a dad. Then one day, her mother had decided to investigate the contents of a blue whale's stomach. It was an interesting experiment that no one had done for thousands of years, and Nim's dad, Jack, said that it would have been all right, it should have been safe – but the Troppo Tourists came to make a film of it, shouting and racing their huge pink-and-purple boat around Nim's mother and the whale. The whale panicked and dived, so deep that no one ever knew where or when he came back up again.

Nim's mother never came back up at all.

So Jack packed his baby onto his boat and sailed round and round the world – and finally, when the baby had grown into a very little girl, he found the perfect island where he could do his science and Nim could grow, wild and free like the animals they lived with.

The island had white shell beaches, pale gold sand and tumbled black rocks. It had a fiery mountain with green rainforest on the high slopes and grasslands at the bottom.

There was a pool of fresh water to drink, a waterfall to slide down and a hidden hollow where the grasslands met the beach. That's where Jack built their hut.

Best of all there was a maze of reef guarding the island from everything but the smallest boats, because Jack and Nim didn't want the Troppo Tourists or anyone else to find their island. But one day, Jack and his boat got lost in a storm – and Nim's email friend, Alex Rover, the most famous and cowardly adventure writer in the whole world, came to rescue Nim.

And then Nim's most secret wish came true: Jack came floating back, and Alex stayed.

Chapter 1

IN A PALM TREE, on an island, in the middle of the wide blue sea, was a girl.

Nim's hair was wild, her eyes were bright, and around her neck she wore three cords. One was for a spyglass, one for a whirly, whistling shell and the other a fat red pocketknife in a sheath.

With the spyglass at her eye, Nim watched the little red seaplane depart. It sailed out through the reef to the deeper dark ocean, bumping across the waves till it was tossed into the bright blue sky. Then it rose so high and so far it was nothing but a speck, and floated out of sight.

'Alex is gone,' Nim told Fred.

Fred stared at the coconuts clustered on the trunk.

Fred was an iguana, spiky as a dragon, with a cheerful snub nose. He was sitting on Nim's shoulder, but he cared more about coconuts than he did about saying goodbye. (Marine iguanas don't eat coconut, but no one had ever told Fred.)

As Nim threw three ripe coconuts *thump* into the sand, she remembered Alex saying, 'I never knew anything could taste better than coffee!' the first time Nim opened a coconut for her.

Nim looked down at her father, sitting like a stone on Selkie's Rock. Jack's head was bowed and his shoulders slumped. Nim had never seen him look so alone.

And she knew she'd made a terrible, terrible mistake, worse than anything she'd ever done before.

～

THE FIRST MISTAKE was when she answered Alex's very first email, back when she'd thought that the famous Alex Rover was a man and a Hero like the hero in his books. That had been a good mistake because when Alex ended up on the island, Jack and Nim wanted her never to leave. Sometimes it felt good to be three instead of two.

But other times Nim wanted Jack just for herself, the way it used to be, and sometimes she wanted Alex just for herself, because Alex was *her* friend before she was Jack's. Sometimes, when Alex and Jack told Nim to go to sleep while they talked late in the night, Nim felt left out and more lonely than she'd ever been when they were two.

And then, this morning, the little red seaplane had arrived with all the things that Alex had asked her editor in the city to send. It was the first time a plane had ever landed on Nim's island. Nim could see Jack was worried that the pilot would notice how beautiful the island was and would want to come back again and again.

Whenever Jack was worried, Nim was too. And when Nim was worried, so were Selkie and Fred. (Selkie was a sea lion, and sometimes she forgot that Nim was a girl and not a little sea lion pup to be looked after and whuffled over.) They both stuck close to Nim every time she walked back and forth from the plane to the hut.

'I've never seen animals do that before!' exclaimed the pilot.

Nim didn't know what to say, partly because she didn't know exactly what he hadn't seen before, and partly because she'd never spoken to anyone except Jack and Alex. She grabbed a crate and opened it up. Inside there were books. Thin books and fat, short books and tall, history books and science, mysteries and fairy tales. Nim didn't know what to read first.

'Come on,' said Alex. 'There'll be time to read when everything's off the plane.'

The pilot pulled out two big solar panels. 'Great!' Jack exclaimed, because he wanted them for the new room he planned to add – one especially for Alex to write her books. Jack balanced the panels on his head and walked very slowly and carefully up to the hut.

'Who's going to take this one?' the pilot asked, pointing to a crate. Nim stepped forward. But just as she was about to reach for the crate, the pilot handed it to Alex. First Alex stumbled, then she tripped, then *crash!* the crate fell to the sand with a tinkle of broken glass.

'Oh, *no*!' Alex wailed. 'What have I done?'

'Jack's test tubes!' Nim shouted. 'You should have let me take it!'

'I was trying to help!'

'But I didn't need help! You just got in the way!'

'I'm always in the way,' Alex snapped. 'Maybe you and Jack would be better off without me.'

'Maybe we would!' Nim shouted, and stomped off without waiting for an answer.

She's right! Alex thought. Nim and Jack lived here perfectly happily all those years without anyone else – they don't really need me. Nim's been cross with me a lot lately and I've never seen Jack so worried. I think...I think I'm changing their lives too much. What if they've secretly been wanting their old lives back – and are too nice to say so?

Alex understood about being afraid to say so. Before she came to the island, she was so afraid of saying anything to anyone that she'd hardly ever left her apartment. She was famous, but only through her books. Her life had changed completely since she flew across the world to find Nim.

'Last one!' The pilot handed her a large envelope. 'And, now, time for me to go.'

Alex opened it and pulled out a letter. 'Wait! Can I... can I go with you?'

'Sure!' he said. 'But don't you need to pack anything?'

Alex knew that if she saw Jack or Nim she would never be able to leave, even if it was the right thing to do. 'No,' she said, 'I'm ready to go.'

She climbed into the little red seaplane. And was gone.

~

NIM SCRAMBLED DOWN from the coconut palm and buried her face in Selkie's warm neck, because the sea lion loved her no matter how bad Nim was – and the feeling in Nim's stomach told her this was the very worst thing she'd ever done.

Jack loved her too, but Nim didn't know if he still would when he realised it was Nim who had chased Alex away.

'Meet me at the Emergency Cave,' she told Selkie, because suddenly the sun and sea were much too bright. Only the deepest, darkest cave could match the way she felt inside.

Selkie gave a disapproving sort of *hrumph*, and lolloped down to the sea. Nim and Fred headed inland, towards the bottom of Fire Mountain, past the Hissing Stones and across the Black Rocks.

Scrambling up the boulders was good because it was such hard work Nim couldn't think about anything else.

But when she got to the cave, she remembered: Alex telling her stories when they were trying to sleep on the hard cave floor, Alex watching the sun rise on the very first morning, Alex crying when Nim skinned her knee.

Nim crawled into the deepest corner of the cave to be as alone as she could possibly be. She hiccupped and coughed and cried and blew her nose, and dropped her hanky.

When she was feeling around in the dark for her soggy hanky, she found a map.

It was the map Alex had drawn when she told one of her stories: a map of an island that was a city with an even bigger city on the land behind. It was as different from Nim's island as anywhere could be.

That's where Alex's books were published, in a tall, shining building whose top floors were up above the clouds. That's where Alex's editor was – the one who'd sent the supply plane that Alex had just left on.

Nim stuffed the map into her deepest pocket and started crying all over again. She cried so hard that Selkie pulled herself all the way up from the sea to the cave to comfort her. But when Nim wouldn't stop crying, no matter how much Selkie whuffled and snuffled, Selkie went outside to do tricks to make her laugh. She balanced a rock on her nose, threw it up in the air and off the cliff. She sat up high on her tail and flapped her flippers as if she were trying to fly. She did a handstand on her front flippers. She went through all her tricks over and over and barked at Nim in between to make her stop crying.

Finally Selkie produced her best trick ever – a handstand right on the edge of the rocks, then a flip into a perfect dive all the way down to the water.

It was a long way down, and it was a very good trick – but Nim didn't come out to see.

And so Nim also didn't see the giant cruise ship that had come around the point and anchored not far from the cliffs.

She didn't see the inflatable motorboat with people snorkelling around it, or the second motorboat chugging quietly out from the other side of the ship. She didn't see the man watching Selkie do her tricks through his binoculars, lift his rifle and shoot Selkie with a tranquilliser dart.

She didn't see him instruct his crew to heave Selkie into his boat and speed away with her to their ship.

BUT FRED DID.

Fred *had* been watching Selkie and hoping she'd do his favourite flipping-a-coconut-high-off-the-cliffs-*smash!*-onto -the-rocks trick. When she did the handstand-dive he ran to the edge of the cliff to see if she'd smashed a coconut on her way down.

What he saw made Fred forget all about coconuts.

First he scrambled down, then he scrambled back up. Then he rushed into the cave and headbutted Nim's leg. When she still didn't pay attention he climbed onto her shoulder and sneezed his cool salt-water spray in her face.

'Yuck, Fred!' said Nim, but when Fred scurried to the edge of the cliff, Nim followed.

The boat was heading back to the ship. Through her spyglass Nim could see Selkie at the bottom of the boat.

'They've killed her!' Nim screamed.

But then Selkie lifted her head, and Nim saw the men tying ropes and nets around her.

She had to save her friend fast.

Fred scrambled to her shoulder and clung on tight. Nim stood on the edge of the cliff. The water was a long way down.

What if I hit the rocks? Nim thought.

She jumped, as high and far as she could, and twisted into a dive.

She hit the water.

Nim's lungs were bursting and her ears were hurting. Then she saw the light above her head, and kicked and spluttered her way up to the air.

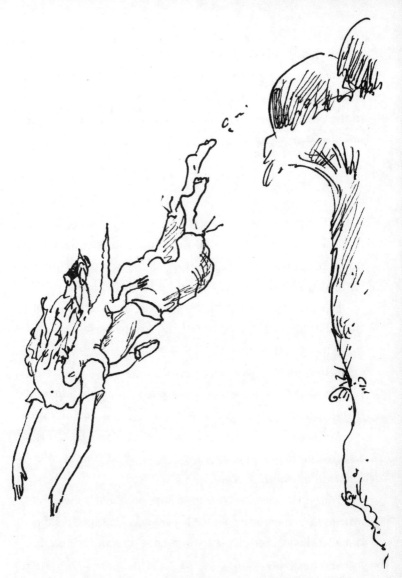

The boat was already a long way out, and the waves were strong on this side of the island, but Nim had no choice. She took another deep breath and began to swim.

Chapter 2

JACK SAT ON Selkie's Rock for a long, long time, staring out at the empty sky. He felt as if half his world had gone up with Alex's plane, and that he'd been left behind.

He reread the letter he'd found on the beach: the letter she'd left behind instead of writing a note herself.

Dear Alex

I'm glad the materials I organised for the supply ship were useful; I hope these things will all be, too. I guess that new cabin must be just about finished by now, and you've all got clothes to wear again. It was quite amusing to read about your banana-leaf dress in your first email!

Your apartment and furniture have been sold, as you instructed. I'm enclosing all the paperwork. However, just in case you change your mind about staying on that little island for ever, I'm also enclosing your new passport and credit card to replace the ones you lost.

Now, please find enclosed the reason I've been so busy: the first copy of your new book. I am very proud to be the editor of this book: I think it's wonderful, and we're going all out to make sure it'll be your bestseller ever.

Please let me know if there's anything else I can do.

Yours,

Delia Defoe

'Why would she…?' said Jack. But no matter how many times he read the letter, it still didn't explain why Alex had gone.

'Could she have changed her mind about selling her apartment?' he asked the sea. 'Did she suddenly want to go and be famous? And why couldn't she tell me?'

But the sea didn't answer, and it didn't matter what Jack wondered, because Alex was gone – and soon he'd have to tell Nim, which would be almost worse than knowing it himself.

Jack was certain he knew exactly where Nim was. He'd seen her face when she'd opened that big crate of books: she'd be lying somewhere, her head on Selkie's back and Fred curled on her stomach, lost in a story, not even realising that everything had changed.

~

ALEX SAT IN the passenger seat of the seaplane, too frozen with sadness to even be afraid. She looked back at the gold sand of Turtle Beach, the black Sea Lion Rocks, the palm tree Nim always climbed and the shack they'd just built, and she wondered if she was making a terrible mistake.

Then she thought about what Nim had said, and knew she cared too much about her friends to stay if Nim didn't want her.

~

FRED JUMPED OFF Nim's shoulder when they hit the water, but he only stayed under long enough to grab one big mouthful of seaweed before popping out beside her.

Selkie was part of Fred's life, and Fred wanted her back.

They were both swimming as fast as they could, straight out to sea, but the boat was pulling away faster. Nim's heart was pounding; it hurt when she breathed and she was swallowing water faster than she could spit it out.

I…*huff*…can't…go…*huff*…fast enough! she thought. She rolled onto her back. Fred kept on gliding under the water just beside her.

When Nim had caught her breath and rolled over again, the cruise ship was getting closer – but the motorboat with Selkie and the seal-nappers had disappeared.

It can't have gone! Nim thought. It must be on the other side of the ship.

That was when she saw the huge pink-and-purple name on the ship's bow: THE TROPPO TOURIST.

The company that Nim and Jack hated more than anything in the world.

Nim tried to swim faster, but it didn't take long before she was gasping and swallowing water again. She rolled to her back again; her arms whirred, her legs kicked…and her head knocked hard against a rubber boat.

Hands grabbed her arms. A man and a woman, with horrified faces and matching pink-and-purple T-shirts, stared down at her.

'Fred!' screamed Nim.

Fred scrabbled to her shoulder and they were hauled into an inflatable motorboat like the one that had seal-napped Selkie.

'You said you'd counted!' shouted the woman whose T-shirt said I'M KYLIE.

'I did!' The man named Kelvin answered. 'There were fifteen kids in that snorkelling group and we took fifteen back. I think.'

'If you'd counted,' Kylie insisted, 'we wouldn't be fishing this poor kid out of the water just before the ship is set to sail!'

'Maybe she's a castaway from that deserted island. We've found Kid Crusoe!'

'You're not funny,' Kylie snapped.

Nim didn't have enough breath to say her name was Nim Rusoe, not Kid Crusoe.

'Where were you heading to, kid?'

'To the boat,' Nim whispered.

She still couldn't see the other little boat. All she could see was the cruise ship: its white length stretching for ever in front of her, and its towering decks reaching to the sky.

It was the only place Selkie's boat could have come from, and the only place it could have gone. If Nim was going to rescue Selkie, she had to get on this ship.

Fred sneezed.

'What *is* that?' Kelvin demanded.

'I don't care what it is – throw it back!'

Fred clung tight to Nim and glared his fiercest dragon glare. 'He's my friend!' Nim shouted.

'If you say so,' Kelvin grinned. He didn't look as if he really wanted to touch Fred anyway.

'She's delirious.'

'We'd better let her keep it.'

'Where's your snorkel, honey?'

'I don't know,' said Nim.

'Never mind,' said Kylie, with a big phoney smile. 'We won't tell anyone you lost a valuable snorkel if you don't tell anyone you nearly missed the boat.'

'Great idea!' said Kelvin. 'Look, kid, we don't want to get you into trouble. Your parents would be pretty mad if they found out you hadn't stayed with the other kids the way you were supposed to.'

'You'd probably be grounded all the way to New York City!'

'Stuck in your cabin for six whole days – you wouldn't like that, would you?'

Nim felt as if her head was going to explode. 'Where's *Selkie*?' she shouted.

'Who's Selkie?'

'We haven't lost another kid, have we?'

'She's a…' But Nim stopped just before she said 'sea lion'. She remembered the part in Alex's book when the Hero tricked the Bad Guys out of kidnapping him because they thought he was crazy.

'…a mermaid,' said Nim.

'She's had too much sun!'

'Too long in the water!'

'Wrap her up – grab that jacket.'

Kelvin dropped a pink-and-purple Troppo jacket over Nim and Fred. He still didn't seem to want to touch Fred.

Kylie looked at him the way Selkie glared at Fred when he ate Nim's lunch. 'Don't worry, kiddo, I'll get you settled down before you see your parents; you'll be fine!'

The boat bumped against the ship. A long plank with rope railings led up from the water to a door halfway along the side. Kelvin grabbed a rope, and Kylie pushed Nim up the ramp and onto the ship.

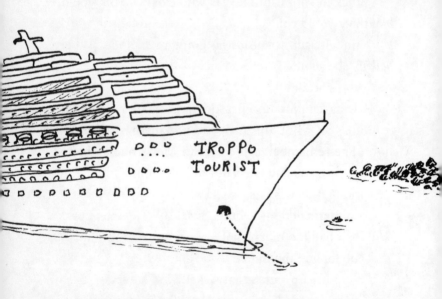

Chapter 3

NIM WAS IN a big open room with small palm trees and large, bright flowers. There were decks above her, a long hall lined with doors leading off to the left, and a white stone fountain to the right. And everywhere she looked there were people: sitting on the edge of the fountain, looking out over the rail, relaxing in deck chairs, perched at small tables with drinks and snacks, sitting at desks across from beaming Troppo Tourist crew members. They were talking and laughing and smiling and scowling and gazing around.

Nim froze.

'Are you okay?' Kylie asked sharply.

Nim nodded, but she could hardly breathe. She took a step closer to the fountain where water bubbled and splashed from the mouth of a carved stone dolphin. In the tiny pool around it were two dolphins swimming in endless circles.

Nim gasped. The dolphins she knew swam free and far across the sea – but these animals barely had room to splash.

'This way,' Kylie said, quickly steering Nim down a flight of stairs and into another long hallway with a shiny green floor, and walls lined with doors. There were no windows, and even though light shone from bright lamps in the ceiling, Nim felt as closed-in as if she were in a cave. Fred curled himself tightly around her neck, peering out from under her chin.

Kylie pulled out a key, unlocked the door marked 12 and pushed Nim into a cabin. There were two bunk beds, two sets of drawers, and a door into a tiny, shiny room. She reached in and handed Nim a towel.

'You'd better get warm and dry before you go back to the Kids' Klub,' she said. 'Were you supposed to have lunch with your mum and dad?'

'No,' said Nim.

'Well, how about I get you something yummy? What about a hamburger and milkshake? A bit of lunch and you'll feel all better.'

'I don't know,' said Nim.

Kylie's smile got even bigger and phonier. 'You'll be fine, you'll see!' She stepped out the door, called, 'Have a shower if you want; that'll warm you up!' and disappeared.

Nim waited a second, and tried to open the door.

The door wouldn't open.

Nim had lived all her life on the island. She'd read about locks, but she'd never seen one. She'd never known what it would be like to be inside a small room and not be able to get out. She pulled the knob and kicked the door as hard as she could.

'Ow!' she shouted, rubbing her big toe.

'Now what do we do?' she asked Fred.

Fred felt braver now that Kylie was gone. He crawled down from Nim's shoulder and began to explore. In the tiny room behind the door he'd found an even tinier room with glass walls and a hard floor with a hole in the middle. Alex had told Nim about toilets that flushed and showers like waterfalls that ran as hot or as cold as you liked. When Nim wanted to get clean she swam in the sea or soaked in the rainforest pool. But now she turned the tap on – and the water gushed out just like Alex said, warm as sunshine.

'I'll try it if you will!' she told Fred.

Nim stuck her arm under the spray, then her leg, and then she and Fred jumped back and forth under the water and out the door, till there were puddles on the floor, splashes up the walls and drops on the ceiling. Fred got so hot he couldn't stay still, and raced crazily around the cabin and up and down the bunks till he was worn out. Nim turned the tap off, rubbed her hair with the towel and shook herself to dry her clothes.

She was wearing the blue shirt and red pants made with the material from the supply ship. Jack had designed the pants with drawstring legs that could be pushed up into shorts for coolness or pulled down smooth for swimming or palm-tree-climbing. There were lots of pockets for Useful Things, including one extra deep pocket with its own drawstring to keep special things safe. Nim pushed the legs up into shorts now, because they were soggy and dripping.

Everything else in the bathroom was soggy too, and quite a lot of things in the cabin – especially the pillow Fred was stretched out on.

The door opened, and Kylie came in with a tray piled with food. Her face went pale when she saw the cabin. 'I see you had a shower!' she exclaimed with a forced little laugh. 'I bet you feel better now!'

'A little bit,' Nim said.

'Well, this ought to fix it. Look what I've brought you: milkshake, hamburger, chips, some jelly and cake and banana for dessert, and a hot chocolate in case you're still cold.'

'Thank you,' said Nim. She stared at the food and

wondered what to try first: the banana was the only thing she recognised. She put it in her pocket when Kylie wasn't looking.

'Those are interesting shorts you're wearing,' Kylie said. 'I thought they were a wetsuit.'

'They're wet shorts,' Nim explained. She opened the hamburger and found some lettuce. Something else I know! Nim thought, but Fred snatched it and gulped it down. She'd have to try the strange foods.

The milkshake slid cold down her throat, and then hot chocolate warmed it up again. Nim tried a mouthful of slippery green jelly. She liked the way it squished it through her teeth. She ate a handful of hot salty chips, and the pickle from the hamburger. Fred did too. Fred liked the jelly best. Nim liked the hot chocolate. And the salty chips. It was hard to decide.

Kylie watched Nim and Fred trying the food, mouthful by mouthful. 'That's an interesting way to eat,' she said.

'It's interesting food,' Nim said politely.

Suddenly there was a faint rumble from somewhere deep inside the ship, and the floor beneath Nim's bare feet began a steady, chugging tremble. The ship's engines had started.

If I don't get out of here, thought Nim, it'll be too late!

'Do you feel well enough to go back to the Kids' Klub?'

Nim nodded. She had to start looking for Selkie somewhere.

'Do you want to take that – I mean, your friend – with you?'

Fred rushed to the plate, slurped down the last of the jelly and raced up to Nim's shoulder. Nim picked up a pink-and-purple jacket. She thought a disguise might be useful. She threw the jacket over Fred on her shoulder so he was disguised too, all except for his watching eyes and iguana grin.

They followed Kylie down the hall to a fish tank with a sign that said PIRANHA DECK. Nim held Fred's tail to make extra sure he didn't fall in.

Kylie stopped and pressed a button on the wall opposite the tank. Doors slid open, and she ushered Nim and Fred into a small empty room. All that was in it was a doormat that said THURSDAY, a mirror on the wall to see their own frightened faces, and a row of buttons beside the door with a picture of an animal on each one. Kylie pressed the ARMADILLO button and the doors slid shut.

Nim knew about elevators: Alex had told her about her home, an apartment building that was half as high as Fire Mountain, with elevators that took her up and down if she ever wanted to go out. What Nim didn't know was that the elevator would leave her stomach down at the bottom while it whisked the rest of her up to the top. Fred didn't know either. He was so surprised he sneezed his last mouthful of jelly all over Nim's neck.

'Yuck, Fred!' said Nim. It was the first completely true thing she'd said since she'd got on the ship.

'I bet your friends will be glad to see you,' Kylie said, as the elevator stopped.

The only friends Nim had ever had were Selkie and Fred, plus Chica the sea turtle and Galileo the frigate bird – but Chica only came ashore once a year to lay her eggs and Galileo was only your friend if you had a fish in your hand. So for just a minute Nim thought, Selkie's here!

But when the elevator doors opened, the sign said ARMADILLO DECK, and the cage beneath it held two little armadillos rolled into tight armour-plated balls.

Kylie turned, and Nim followed her towards a swimming pool. Selkie wasn't in it, or in the little pool behind it with spray that fountained up like water through the rocks of her own Keyhole Cove. They walked on, past a door marked TROPPO TEENS, past another marked TROPPO TOTS, and opened the KIDS' KLUB door.

Inside, people were making things at tables, others were playing games on giant computer screens, some were running and others were talking; some were bigger than Nim and some smaller. They were as crowded and noisy as seagulls on a beach – and, except for another Troppo Tourist woman whose pink-and-purple T-shirt said KRISTIE, they were all…

…Kids! Nim thought. I didn't think there'd be this many kids in a whole city!

Kylie pushed her firmly into the room, and pulled Kristie out the door. 'Not quite right in the head,' Nim heard her say. 'She shouldn't have been allowed to go snorkelling – and look at the lizard she caught out there! We couldn't get it away from her.'

145

'Never mind – the Professor can deal with that.'

Nim wasn't listening.

In the books Nim had read, kids had adventures together; sometimes they were friends at the beginning of the story and other times they fought and ended up friends in the end. But how are you supposed to know what to do, Nim wondered, when you can't even figure out what they're doing – and they don't even notice you?

She backed against the wall and watched them as if they were a flock of birds that weren't used to her yet.

A girl in front of one of the giant computer screens stopped spinning her steering wheel and looked right at Nim. She smiled, and Nim tried to smile back. The girl came over.

'I'm Erin. Did you get on at that port two days ago, too? I thought we were the only ones.' She pointed to a slightly smaller dark-haired boy who was riding a strange sort of motorbike that kept bouncing him off the seat but didn't go anywhere. 'That's Ben.'

Fred stuck his head out from under the jacket and sneezed.

'Cool!' said Erin. 'What's his name?'

Suddenly a bunch of kids were around them, so close Nim could hardly breathe, asking questions so fast no one even noticed she wasn't answering.

'Where'd you get that thing?'

'Can I touch it?'

'What *is* it?'

'How come the Professor let you have it?'

Fred sneezed again, harder, and they jumped back.

Kristie came back inside and the kids turned to her.

'Look what the Professor gave her!'

'Of course!' Kristie exclaimed. 'You must be the Professor's kid!'

Nim didn't know what a Professor's kid was, but she knew that it might be the disguise that would let her save Selkie.

'All right then, why don't you tell us about your little friend here?'

'He's a marine iguana,' Nim began. 'He can swim and dive…'

'Does he do tricks?'

'Show us some tricks!'

Nim thought fast. Fred could do lots of things. He could gulp down coconut so fast he wouldn't even notice a pearl inside. He could play coconut soccer. He could sink like a stone to the bottom of Keyhole Cove. He could ride on Nim's shoulder and sneeze on her neck.

'Ladies and Gentlemen!' she began, imitating Alex's best story-telling voice, 'Allow me to present: *Fred!*'

Fred stuck his head out from behind her neck to see why she was calling him, saw all the people staring, and stared back even harder.

It wasn't exactly a trick, but: 'Fred here is a champion starer,' said Nim. 'He can stare hard enough to make anyone look away!'

'Not me!' said a red-haired boy. He came closer and stared into Fred's eyes. Fred stared back. The boy moved closer. Fred sneezed.

'Gross!' shouted the boy, and jumped back into the crowd.

Everyone laughed and clapped.

'Thank you, Fred!' said Nim. 'What would you like to do for your next trick?'

Fred stared at her. His mouth opened and shut as if he was eating.

'I don't have any coconut,' said Nim.

Fred brought his face right up to hers and stared harder.

Everyone laughed again. 'Does he really understand?' asked a girl in a sunflower hat.

'No,' said Kristie. 'I went to the Professor's lecture on reptiles and he said they don't understand language.'

'Is he really hungry?' Erin asked Nim.

'Fred's always hungry,' said Nim.

Erin reached for a plate of fruit on a table and held out a segment of mandarin. Fred snatched, started to gulp – and spat mashed mandarin across the room.

Kids jumped, yelled and laughed. All except Erin, and Ben, who'd finally got off the jolting motorbike and was watching quietly.

'I'm sorry, Fred!' Erin said, and gave him a kiwi fruit. Fred didn't like kiwi fruit either. Chomps of green mush flew across the room and everyone laughed harder. Erin looked as if she was going to cry.

'He likes strawberries,' said Nim.

Erin grabbed a strawberry, Fred gulped it down – and didn't spit it out.

Everyone clapped.

'Fred has lots of other tricks,' said Nim, 'but he mostly does them with another performer. He needs to go rehearse with her now.'

Fred settled himself back on her shoulder, and Nim marched out the door.

Oh, Selkie! she thought. Where are you?

Chapter 4

JACK STILL HADN'T moved. He still couldn't believe that Alex had gone, and still couldn't figure out what to say to Nim. 'Let her be happy a little longer,' he decided, and went on staring out at the empty sea.

~

ALEX WAS STILL frozen in her seat, clutching the envelope the pilot had handed her just before she'd jumped on board.

She knew it held the first copy of her new book, and she wasn't ready to see it yet. There was also a credit card, passport, and a thick contract saying that her apartment and furniture had been sold. She'd asked Delia to do that, but she was surprised that there was no letter explaining it.

Just as she remembered that there *had* been a letter and realised she must have dropped it as she climbed on board, the little red seaplane bumped gently down onto the waves and pulled up beside the Sunshine Island wharf. Alex wiped her eyes and climbed out.

It was three months since she'd landed here on her way to find Nim. She'd been nervous then, afraid of flying, afraid of crowds, afraid of the sea – yet it had been exciting too, because she'd been turning into someone new. But if Nim didn't want her on the island any more, there was nothing to do but go home.

Except that, according to the contract she'd just read, she didn't have a home.

'You have to go somewhere!' she told herself.

'Can you take me to the airport on Isla Grande when you've refuelled?' she asked the pilot. He shook his head.

'I'm afraid my old plane needs more than fuel after such a long flight. She'll have to be completely serviced before I take her anywhere else.'

'Howabout when you're finished?'

'It'll be too dark,' the pilot said. 'I'm not an adventurer like you, Alex Rover! The Sunshine Island Seaplane and I don't fly at night.'

'Okay,' said Alex. 'I guess I'll have to find the pilot who flew me here from the big island before.' She took a bus to the little airport.

'Sorry, miss,' the man in the terminal office said. 'The Thursday flight to Isla Grande left half an hour ago. We won't be going again till Tuesday.'

'Five days!' Alex exclaimed. 'I can't wait that long!'

'Well, there's a cruise ship coming in this afternoon.'

'I'll take it,' said Alex.

'It's going all the way to New York City if you like.'

'I'd like,' said Alex.

As the man processed her ticket, Alex looked around the terminal. In a little bookstore just across from her she saw a sign:

COMING SOON:
THE NEWEST BOOK BY ALEX ROVER!
NO DETAILS REVEALED UNTIL
PUBLICATION DATE: **JULY 7!**
BUY IT HERE SOON!

'What's the name on the ticket?' the man asked.

'Al…' Alex looked at the sign again, and shuddered. 'Alice. Alice Dozer.'

She signed for it quickly, so he didn't notice that it wasn't exactly the same name on her credit card.

Then she went to the dock to wait for the ship.

~

'IT'S SIMPLE,' Nim told Fred. 'All we have to do is search the ship, and we'll find Selkie.'

The Kids' Klub was in the stern, so they walked past the elevator and the long rows of locked cabin doors to the set of stairs and elevators up front in the bow.

'Up or down?' Nim asked Fred.

Fred couldn't decide, but the animal buttons outside the elevator showed that the Armadillo Deck was the tenth

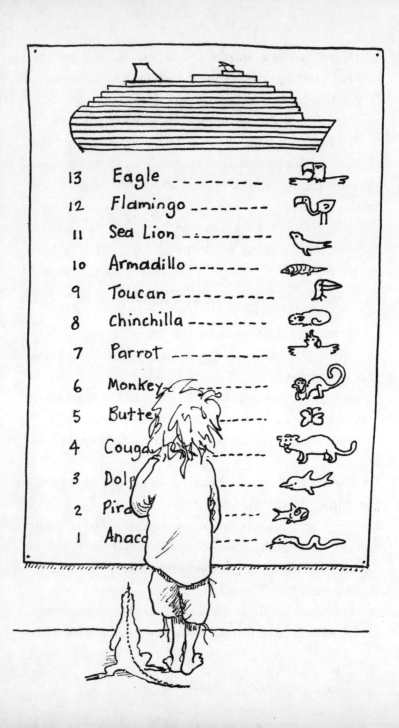

deck above the water, and there were only three more decks above it. The next level up was the Sea Lion Deck.

Aha! Nim thought, and raced up the stairs.

They came out into bright sunshine and saw a small pool with a flat rock in the middle and a wall around the edge saying SEA LION DECK.

There were no sea lions inside it.

Grabbing her shell whistle, Nim blew two long shrill notes that would call Selkie in from the farthest reef at home on the island.

But Selkie didn't come. Nim looked for her in the huge swimming pool with the long curving waterslide, and in the hot bubbling pool where people lazed the way Nim liked to float in her own rainforest pool. The only sea lions she could find anywhere were plastic, set out on a giant chessboard with other life-sized animal pieces.

And beyond the ship, whichever way Nim looked, there was nothing but empty sea. Her island was far, far away.

'Even if we find her,' she said to Fred, 'how are we going to get home?'

Fred stared hard.

'You're right!' Nim said. 'The important thing is to find her – we can figure out how to escape once we're all together.'

The next deck up was the Flamingo, where two long-legged pink birds stood in a shallow pond inside their narrow cage. People at white tables sipped drinks while others whooshed screaming down the waterslide into the

Sea Lion Deck pool. Nim thought about how much Selkie would love the slide. Fred tickled under her chin to say he'd like to try it, too.

Upstairs, at the very top of the ship, there was only a half deck, where joggers in shorts ran on a track through an aviary of eagles.

'So now we have to go down,' Nim said. She decided to take the elevator – and even though her stomach still flip-flopped, it wasn't quite so bad now that she knew it was going to happen.

They went down past the Flamingo and Sea Lion Decks, past the Armadillo Deck where the Kids' Klub was, and got out on the Toucan Deck. It had a path outside, where people leaned over the railing to gaze out to sea, and inside it was full of cabins, with a hall down the middle.

In every hall was a cage with the animals the deck was named after. After the toucan were chinchillas, and then parrots, but the one that made Nim feel the saddest and sickest of all was the cage with six frightened baby spider monkeys.

But on the Monkey Deck, down the outside path on each side of the ship, was a row of lifeboats hoisted high on strong steel frames, with a cover like a little roof on top of each one. Most were big enough to hold lots of people, but in the middle was a small, inflatable motorboat, like the one that had picked her up this morning, with a canvas cover on top. Exactly like the one that had seal-napped Selkie.

Nim whistled her shell whistle again, loud and clear

under the boat, and again under the one on the other side of the ship.

There was no answer, not the slightest thump or whuffle.

Nim ran on down to the Butterfly Deck, which was full of rooms with things to buy, and rooms with food and drink – but most of all, full of people. Men and women, old and young, fat and thin, bald and hairy, in bathing suits and white uniforms, in shorts and T-shirts and long silk dresses. People, people, people! Nim thought. It was like being in the middle of sunbaking sea lions, but noisier.

She opened a door to a library full of books and quiet, but she couldn't hide there until she'd found Selkie. Behind another door, amidst a room of smiling people, a woman with a long white dress and flowers in her hair was walking up the aisle to a man who looked so happy he was nearly crying.

A wedding! Nim thought. I'm seeing a real wedding!

She felt like crying too, but not because she was happy.

Nim and Fred looked in cafés and restaurants, beauty salons and barbershops, dress shops and pyjama shops, sports shops and toy shops. On the next deck, they watched a cougar snarling as it paced its cramped cage in a room with bright lights and red velvet. They searched in video arcades, piano bars and theatres. They were back down on the deck where they'd come on board, but there was still no sign of Selkie.

Fred rubbed his spiky back against Nim's neck.

'You're right,' she said. 'We'll find her. We just have to keep going.'

~

DOWN THE STAIRS Nim ran, past the Piranha Deck where Kylie's cabin was, down to the lowest deck of all.

There weren't any people on this deck; the engine's deep rumble was louder and thumped more strongly through her feet, with a smell that reminded her of the seaplane. And instead of a painting of an animal at the bottom of the stairs, this sign said:

CREW ONLY! NO PASSENGERS ALLOWED!

Nim put on her Troppo Tourist jacket.

A man in grey overalls came out of a doorway. 'What are you doing here?' he demanded.

'I'm…I'm taking him back to the Professor,' Nim said, pointing to Fred on her shoulder.

'His door's behind you.'

'Thanks!' said Nim, hoping he wouldn't hear her heart, which was thumping as hard as her feet on the steel floor. She turned to the door that said:

FOUNDATION FOR RESEARCH ON INTELLIGENT, UNIQUE AND INTERESTING ANIMALS DANGER: KEEP OUT.

Nim went in.

Chapter 5

THE ROOM WAS full of cages and sad smells. There were parrots, songbirds, lizards, spider monkeys, a tank of tropical fish – and Selkie, lying in a cage beside an old bathtub full of dirty seawater.

Nim raced across the room, yanked open the cage door and threw herself onto the sea lion, hugging and kissing her, rubbing her head and tickling her whiskers. Selkie whuffled and opened her eyes.

'It's okay, Selkie,' Nim whispered. 'I've come to –' but before she could finish the sentence, a deep voice snarled, 'Hey! What are you doing here?'

Nim looked up at a tall pale man with steel blue eyes. Nim didn't recognise him, but Jack would have, and so would Alex. The Professor had been on the Troppo Tourist boat that scared Nim's mother's whale to the bottom of the sea, and on the one that had dropped off Alex and her tiny boat in the terrible storm when Jack was lost at sea and Alex came to rescue Nim.

All Nim knew was that he was the person who'd

seal-napped Selkie. She was as angry as Fire Mountain before it erupted.

But she also knew she'd never get Selkie out of here if she let that fire escape.

'Are you the Professor?' she asked.

He nodded. 'How did you get down here?'

'I want to work with the animals,' said Nim.

The Professor laughed. 'Let me guess: your mum's on the crew, she smuggled you on board, and now you're bored!'

Nim nodded as if he'd guessed her secret.

'What's your mum's name?'

'Alex,' said Nim, and then she felt even worse. Her mother's name had been Joni.

'And will she think it's a good idea for you to be snooping around down here?'

'She knows I like learning about animals,' Nim said quickly. 'And...and I thought you'd like to see this marine iguana.'

Fred stared fiercely.

'That,' said the Professor, 'is the ugliest thing I've ever seen.

Luckily, some people like ugly. Find an empty cage and stick it in.'

Fred tucked himself tighter around Nim's neck.

'HE'S NOT GOING IN A CAGE!' Nim said. 'Animals don't belong in cages!'

The Professor's voice was like ice. 'The Foundation for Research into Intelligent, Unique and Interesting Animals helps animals from all over the world. The most intelligent, unique or interesting will go to millionaires' homes – I mean, be relocated in appropriate environments – at the end of the cruise.'

'But…the iguana could learn to be even more intelligent, unique and interesting if he stays with me!'

The Professor shrugged. 'Suit yourself – as long as you remember that all the animals on this ship are the property of the Foundation. But if you want to tame him, I guess I can allow that.'

'We've already put on a show for the Kids' Klub.'

He laughed, a thin sort of laugh. 'So you fancy yourself a mini-Professor, do you? Think you could take over my job of giving animal lectures to the passengers?'

'No, no, of course not! It was just a little show for the kids. But I could help you…I've even worked with sea lions before. I bet I could teach that one all sorts of tricks!'

'That sea lion,' the Professor said, 'is a mean, vicious beast. It tried to bite me when I rescued it. It'll be more cooperative after a few days with no food.'

Nim felt as if someone had thrown a coconut hard against her stomach. She took a deep breath. 'Think, think!' she told herself. 'All that matters is helping Selkie!'

'Sea Lion,' she announced to the cage, 'your name is… Selkie! Selkie, come out!'

'You can't do that!' the Professor bellowed as he jumped out of Selkie's way.

'Selkie,' Nim began.

The Professor grabbed a long whip from the corner of the room.

Nim looked around wildly. There was nowhere to hide. 'Don't you hit her!' she screamed, and leapt in front of her friend.

'We'll get out of this somehow,' she whispered to Selkie. 'Just do what I say, even if it seems stupid.'

'Get away from her,' the Professor snarled.

Nim ignored him. 'Selkie: handstand!'

Selkie raised herself on her front flippers, and did her best handstand.

What next? Nim thought, desperately.

Fred scurried across to Selkie. He rolled himself into a ball.

'Oh, Fred!' said Nim.

Fred rolled himself tighter.

'Selkie,' said Nim. 'Soccer!'

Selkie sat thinking with her head on one side, the way she did when something was tricky. Nim always shouted at her when she threw Fred instead of the coconut when they played soccer, and Fred always sulked.

'Soccer!' Nim said again.

Selkie flicked Fred up with her nose, and threw him neatly to Nim. He climbed tight around Nim's neck again.

'Thank you!' said Nim. 'Now, give me a kiss.'

Selkie waddled over and whiskery-kissed Nim on the cheek.

The Professor's eyes opened wide with surprise. He smiled as he put down his whip. 'Okay, girlie, you can help.'

Chapter 6

JACK SAT ON Selkie's Rock till his shadow stretched dark across the beach – but the little red seaplane never came back, and neither did Nim.

'Nim!' Jack called, walking home to the new hut the three of them had built together. Nim and Jack's previous home had been blown away by the terrible storm. 'Nim! Dinner time!'

The only answer was a honk from a sea lion. Jack couldn't tell whether or not it was Selkie.

'Nim!' he called again. 'Nim!'

She wasn't at the hut. She wasn't on Turtle Beach or Shell Beach, or at the rainforest pool or the vegetable garden, or on Sea Lion Rocks at Keyhole Cove.

She knows Alex has gone! Jack thought. She doesn't want to see me because I somehow drove Alex away. Poor Nim!

He climbed up to the Emergency Cave, because he thought she might hide there if she really didn't want to see him.

There were fresh footprints on the floor, but no Nim. And that's when Jack really started to worry.

~

ALEX SAT so long in the Sunshine Island waiting room that the sea outside the window had turned black. Suddenly the ship floated into the harbour with its lights twinkling like a fairy-tale castle.

Alex didn't care about fairy tales. She just wanted to go to her cabin, lock the door, and not come out till she got to the other side of the world.

~

THERE WERE NO portholes in the Animal Room, but Nim felt the engines stop, and the ship bump gently against a wharf.

Now we can escape! Nim thought, rubbing Selkie's head in a get-ready way. Fred was already tucked tight on her shoulder, worn out after his busy day.

'Okay, kid,' said the Professor. 'Time to get that sea lion back into its cage.'

'But…'

The Professor pointed his whip at her. 'Let's get things straight. Out of the goodness of my heart, I'm going to let you help me with the animals. But if you don't do exactly what I say, when I say it, I'll have to tell the Captain that your mum brought a stowaway on board. He'll have to tell the police, and you and Alex will have to go to jail.'

Nim nodded.

Nim hugged Selkie, hard, and it felt like the second worst thing she'd ever done.

Selkie slid slowly into her cage.

'Now, scram. I don't want your mum snooping around here looking for you.'

'She wouldn't do that!' Nim spluttered, though she didn't know if she was defending her mother or Alex.

The Professor laughed, pushed her out the door, and locked it behind him.

There was nothing Nim could do but walk back up the hall and up the stairs as if she knew where she was going.

'Fred,' she whispered, when they were alone. 'What are we going to do?'

Fred made his hungry face, which wasn't any help at all.

Nim got into the elevator, pushed the Armadillo button, and went back to the Kids' Klub. No one was there. Nim and Fred curled up in a chair to share the banana in her pocket – but she'd seen two women cleaning the Troppo Tots' room next door, and Nim knew that if they came in here they'd tell her to get out and go back to her cabin. Even with Fred on her shoulder Nim felt alone, very small, and very, very frightened. She needed to find somewhere safe to sleep.

An empty soft drink bottle rolled out from under a chair.

Nim thought of how she and Jack always checked bottles when they drifted in with the tide. 'There might be a message,' Jack always said. So far, there never had been – but they liked imagining that someday there might be.

Paper and pencils were stacked on a desk. Nim peeked out the door: the women were still washing the Troppo Tots' floor. She had maybe a minute before they found her.

Dear Jack

The Troppo Tourists have seal-napped Selkie.
Fred and I are on the ship too. We will rescue
Selkie as soon as we can but she is locked
up tonight.

I'm very, very sorry I made Alex leave.
Love (as much as Selkie loves fish)
Nim

Nim walked slowly down the stairs to the next deck, around the walkway that ran right around the ship, and then down to the next and the one after that, because she didn't know where to go or what else to do. She could see lights on the wharf and in the houses behind it, as if everyone had a torch or candles in their windows. It looked like a scene out of a fairy tale.

Other people were looking out too, leaning on the railings and chatting. Some of them smiled and said hello, but Nim kept on walking around to the other side of the ship. No one was on that side because there was nothing to look at except the black and empty sea, and nothing to do unless you were a lonely Nim throwing her message-in-a-bottle far into the darkness, hoping the waves would float it to Jack.

She went down the stairs again, to the Monkey Deck, where the lifeboats were. She stopped under the smaller, inflatable motorboat.

'Hang on, Fred,' said Nim.

Swinging upside down like a nimble monkey-girl, Nim scrambled up the frame and onto the boat, unclipped one end of the canvas cover and slid inside. Then she pulled out four life jackets to make a mattress and pillow, and curled up.

Fred went straight to sleep, but Nim kept seeing Selkie locked in her cage, and Alex flying away on the plane, and Jack coming happily back from unloading his solar panels to find Alex gone. She didn't know how she was going to save Selkie, or where they were going to end up, or how they were going to live on this ship.

For the first time since she was a baby, Nim cried herself to sleep.

NIM WAS SO tired, and the canvas lifeboat cover kept the light out so well, that she didn't wake up till long after the sun was up and the ship was back out at sea.

She opened her eyes, peeked quickly over the edge of the lifeboat – and ducked down even faster, because a boy was coming out of the cabin in front of her.

Nim settled back down to wait. Fred made a hungry face, so she dug through all her pockets to see what she could find: a pencil and a very soggy notebook, a green stone, five ankle bands for birds visiting the island, a small bamboo cup, a few strands of seaweed…and the map Alex had drawn.

She gave Fred the seaweed and, very gently, spread Alex's map out on the seat. It was torn on the fold lines and a bit faded.

'You'll be grounded all the way to New York,' Kylie had said when they pulled Nim out of the sea. New York was where Alex's editor was – the one person in the world who would know where Alex was now.

'Oh, Fred, we're going to rescue Selkie, find Alex – and bring us all together again!' she whispered. 'All we have to do is stay on the ship till the end of the trip – without getting caught.'

Then there was a thump, and a bump, and a boy slithered into Nim's boat.

Chapter 7

NIM AND THE boy stared at each other.

Fred and the boy stared at each other.

'Ben!' a girl called. 'What are you doing?'

Ben didn't answer.

'I'm coming up too!'

Nim's boat rocked again, and Erin slithered in.

'Be quiet!' Ben hissed. 'She's a stowaway!'

'I thought you were the Professor's kid!'

'I didn't mean to stow away,' Nim said, 'but the Professor kidnapped Selkie.'

'Kidnapped!' Erin and Ben whispered together, crouching closer towards her in the bottom of the lifeboat.

I shouldn't have told them! Nim thought. Now Selkie will stay in that cage forever.

'Who's Selkie?' asked Erin.

'How are you going to rescue her all by yourself?' asked Ben.

~

SO NIM TOLD them her story. It was hard for Erin and Ben to believe, but they knew it was true.

'We'll help!' said Erin.

'It's not going to be easy,' said Nim. 'We need to make a plan.'

'But first, we all need breakfast,' said Ben. Fred lifted his head and stared. He liked this Ben.

'You exit first, Ben,' said Erin. 'No one's ever surprised to see you popping out of strange places.'

With a quick peek over the edge, Ben swung down, and a second later rapped twice on the metal frame to say the coast was clear. Erin followed. After a while there were two more raps, and Nim climbed out too. Erin was waiting at the open door of the cabin; Nim could see a man and a woman disappearing down the stairs with two small girls and Ben.

'Come inside, quick!' Erin whispered.

This cabin was bigger and fancier than Kylie's, with two beds and two sets of drawers and lamps, a desk and wardrobe.

'This is Ben's and mine,' Erin said. 'Mum and Dad and the twins are in the cabin next door – but they've gone to breakfast now, so we'll be okay.' She opened the wardrobe. 'I've got some clothes for you.'

'I've already got clothes!' said Nim.

'Your shorts are great,' Erin said, 'but if you're going to hide on the ship, you need to look like the other kids.'

Erin was right, Nim thought. A disguise was more important than wearing her own clothes.

In the bathroom, Erin gave Nim a bag with a toothbrush, a tiny tube of toothpaste and a comb. 'We got these on the plane. Meet us at the Kids' Klub after you've visited Selkie – we'll bring you breakfast.'

Erin raced out to meet up with her family, and Nim had a shower. This time she closed the shower door so Fred couldn't run in and out, and not much water got on the floor. She hung her towel up where Erin had shown her, changed into her new clothes, and slipped out of the cabin, her rubber sandals flip-flopping a strange music on her feet.

The Animal Room was still locked. Nim sat outside the door, calling to Selkie through the crack, but she couldn't hear any sea lion whuffles on the other side. Finally, the Professor came to unlock it, yawning and grumbling.

Selkie was sitting up in her cage, looking cross and bored. Nim rushed to her.

'Never hug the animals!' the Professor snarled.

'But it helps them learn tricks,' said Nim.

The Professor grunted. 'So what do you think you could teach them?'

'I'll bet the sea lion could catch fish,' said Nim.

Selkie barked yes.

Nim threw two fish high and twirling, and Selkie caught them both.

'That's enough,' snapped the Professor. 'She needs to be hungry enough to learn something more interesting.'

'She could do much better tricks if she was in the water,' said Nim.

The Professor pointed to the bathtub.

'That's not big enough!' But Selkie slid into it, because if she rolled and splashed at least she could get wet.

'She's just too fat!' the Professor sneered.

Selkie glared and slid out of the tub – and Fred scrabbled from Nim's shoulder into the bit of water left behind, checking for seaweed.

Nim threw a fish into the tub. Fred didn't eat fish, so he flicked it over the edge to Selkie. Selkie opened her mouth, and the fish disappeared.

'If they had a pool to practise in,' said Nim, 'I could teach them fantastic tricks.'

'Hmph,' said the Professor. Nim wished she knew what that 'hmph' meant, but at least he let her give Selkie the rest of her breakfast fish. She put out seeds for the birds, too, and fruit for the monkeys and lizards, but most of the animals cowered at the back of their cages, too frightened to eat.

Fred clung tight to Nim's shoulder. He was too afraid of being locked up to even steal food from the caged lizards.

Selkie stuck close to Nim's side, whuffling worriedly. She was afraid of being locked up again, too, but she was more worried about what the bad man might do to Nim.

And so when the Professor ordered Selkie to her cage and Nim out of the room, Selkie didn't complain so that Nim wouldn't worry, and Nim didn't cry so that Selkie wouldn't worry.

Fred just waited till the Professor had gone the other way down the hall, with the key in his pocket – then he sneezed, hard.

AFTER THE GREY misery of the Animal Room, the Kids' Klub seemed like a strange kind of dream, with too many lights and too many colours, too much noise, and too many kids.

'Come on,' said Erin, 'let's go outside.'

They ran up the stairs to the Sea Lion Deck. 'The perfect spot for planning a sea lion rescue!' Ben exclaimed.

It was hard not to feel a little happier as they lounged in the deck chairs beside the great blue pool, looking out over the deeper blue sea. Erin gave Nim a peanut butter sandwich on fresh white bread. The peanut butter was sticky, but Nim liked it after the first few bites. Ben had a banana in his pocket that was only a little bit squashed, and a piece of watermelon in a napkin that was completely smashed.

Fred loved smashed watermelon.

And as they ate and talked, their plan grew – and grew and grew.

~

ALEX HAD NO plans at all. Not one.

A young woman with *Virginia* on her nametag knocked on the cabin door with a glass of good morning juice. 'I'm your steward for the trip, Miss Dozer – is there anything I can do to help you settle in?'

'Could you have all my meals sent to my cabin, please?'

'Sure!' said Virginia. 'But I hope you're feeling well enough to get out and do things soon. The Professor's lecturing on Spider Monkeys this afternoon. Poor little things…anyway, the Professor says they don't mind being away from their mothers, and he's the expert! Maybe you'll feel well enough to go to that.'

'Maybe,' said Alex. Then she remembered she'd been wearing her same blue T-shirt and red pants for two days and a night. 'Is there anywhere on the ship to buy clothes?'

Virginia smiled. 'Clothes, jewellery, sports gear… we've got absolutely everything!' She handed Alex a phone directory from the desk. 'Do you know there's one old lady who lives on the ship full time? She says she never intends to go ashore again, because the ship has everything a city does – so I'm sure you'll find something you want.'

Alex flipped through the directory, and phoned the Troppo Ladies' Leisurewear Shoppe to order a few new pairs of shorts and tops.

But when she opened her mouth, she heard herself ask for pyjamas, because deep down, all she really wanted to do was stay in her bed from now until she had to get off the ship. Or maybe she'd be like the old lady and just stay on the ship for the rest of her life.

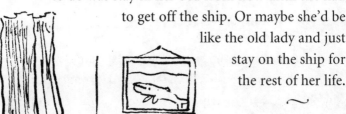

JACK HAD SEARCHED for Nim all night, from one end of the island to the other and across the other side. When the sun came up he was on top of Fire Mountain.

Far below him was the top of Frigate Bird Cliffs, then Turtle Beach's pale gold sand, the grasslands and Shell Beach at the hut, Sea Lion Point and Keyhole Cove, and finally the grim black lava-rock, where the Emergency Cave was hidden.

But no matter which way or how far his binoculars searched, there was no sign of Nim.

'She's not on the island,' Jack finally admitted. 'And Selkie would never let her fall into the sea and drown. She must be with Alex.'

The picture of the seaplane leaving was burned into his mind, but when he tried to decide if he could have seen the top of Nim's wild hair in the back, behind Alex's gold head, sometimes he could and sometimes he just couldn't.

Jack was angry because they'd left without telling him, and he was frightened for Nim because she'd never been in a city, even though she'd be safe with Alex. But most of all he was sad because he was on the island without them and they were somewhere else without him, and they should all be together.

'I'll simply have to go and find them,' said Jack.

The problem was, he had absolutely no idea where they could be.

Chapter 8

TWELVE WEEKS AGO, a storm had taken Jack's boat. The same storm that had brought Alex to the island. The boat never came back – and Jack hadn't yet built a new one.

He'd have to take the seaplane, just like Alex and Nim. With a bit of luck, by the time it got here he'd know where he was going.

Jack ran, slid and skidded, all the way down Fire Mountain back to the hut. He turned on the computer and checked his emails just in case there was one from Alex, and when there wasn't, he wrote one to her.

From: jack.rusoe@explorer.net
To: aka@incognito.net
Date: Friday 2 July, 7:03am
Subject: WHERE ARE YOU?

Dear Alex

    Why did you go? Where have you gone?

    Why did you take Nim without telling me?

    Please give her this message:

Dear Nim

Stay with Alex; I'm coming.

Love, Jack

Then, to make sure Nim knew he meant it, he added,

(as much as Selkie loves the ocean)

Next he wrote:

From: jack.rusoe@explorer.net
To: delia.defoe@papyruspublishing.com
Date: Friday 2 July, 7:05am
Subject: Alex Rover

Dear Delia

Alex has disappeared. She's taken Nim. Do you know where she's gone?

Yours truly,

Jack Rusoe

Finally he wrote:

From: jack.rusoe@explorer.net
To: seaplane@sunshineisland.com
Date: Friday 2 July, 7:08am
Subject: EMERGENCY!

Please return to the island where you brought supplies this morning. I need to leave immediately.

Urgently

Jack Rusoe

The computer dinged before he'd even had time to stand up.

From: delia.defoe@papyruspublishing.com
To: jack.rusoe@explorer.net
Date: Friday 2 July, 7:09am
Subject: Re: Alex Rover

Thank you for your email. I'm presently out of the office due to the preparations for the launch of Alex Rover's exciting new book on July 7. I can assure you, it will be worth the wait!

As you can appreciate, there is a large backlog of emails at this time; however, I will endeavour to reply within ten to fifteen working days.

Regards,

Delia Defoe

'Ten to fifteen working days!' Jack shouted. 'I can't wait that long!'

The computer dinged again.

From: seaplane@sunshineisland.com
To: jack.rusoe@explorer.net
Date: Friday 2 July, 7:10am
Subject: I'm on vacation!

I am going on holidays, so Sunshine Island Seaplane will be closed from Thursday evening, 1st July to Monday 30th August. I hope this doesn't cause any inconvenience.

This is an automated reply. This mailbox will not be checked until Monday 30th August.

Happy travelling!

    Sam

    Sunshine Island Seaplane

'How am I going to travel?' Jack shouted.

'And,' he added, as he typed 'Troppo Tourists' into the search box, 'I'M NOT HAPPY!'

Jack thought their island was the most beautiful island in the whole world, with birds and animals who were free and happy. He had tried to hide it from the Troppo Tourists because he knew that if they came they'd drive away the birds and animals, and pick the plants, and then it wouldn't be the most beautiful island in the world any more.

But here's the thing – Jack loved Nim more than he hated the Troppos. And since they'd once brought Alex nearly all the way from Sunshine Island, maybe they could take him back.

'GOODBYE ADVENTURE CHARTERS! HELLO LUXURY CRUISES! BIGGER AND BETTER IN EVERY WAY!
The Troppo Tourists have said farewell to the charter ship that took you on so many adventurous tours. Why plan a trip yourself when we can do it all for you? Remember: if it's worth seeing, The Troppo Tourist can take you there!

So come and join us on our glorious new luxury cruise ship! Click here for schedules.'

JACK DIDN'T BOTHER reading any more. He switched off the computer.

'Luxury cruises!' he muttered, as he pulled the sleeping mats away from a wall.

The wall was built of strong bamboo poles, firmly laced together. It was the only one without a door or window. Jack grabbed the axe from behind the hut.

'Here's to happy travelling!' he shouted, as he chopped a raft-sized square out of the wall. He nailed a blanket across the hole, to keep out the dust and birds, and dropped an empty bag over the computer and science stuff. 'That'll have to do!' declared Jack.

With a thick rope, he hauled his raft across the sand to Shell Beach. He was hot, tired and thirsty when he finished, but he only stopped long enough to split a coconut and drink its milk. It was strange not to have Fred begging for the coconut meat...

Fred might be on a plane! Jack thought, and he almost smiled as he raced up the hill to Tabletop Garden.

Jack found two strong, slim lengths of bamboo just the right size for a mast and a cross bar, chopped them down and raced back to the beach. He lashed the cross bar to the mast, cut a neat hole out of the centre of his raft and then. with wires and rope and bits of bamboo, fixed the mast in place.

'At least the sail will be easy,' said Jack. He pulled out a bag he'd unloaded from the seaplane just the day before. In it was a sail for the boat he'd planned to build. It was a

perfect, clean white sail, light and strong enough to catch
any wind – but it was too tall and too wide for his little
make-shift raft.

Jack had never had a brand-new sail before.

He took out his fat red pocketknife, cut a big square
from the sail, and rigged it to the mast.

Jack looked out at the wide empty sea and his small-sailed raft. It didn't look very big or very strong.

He stuffed six coconuts, a change of pants and shirt, and his toothbrush into the sail bag, dropped his compass into one pocket and his notebook and pen in another, and grabbed two fishing lines, two big containers of water and some bananas.

Finally, he opened a metal box. It hadn't been opened for a long, long time, but his wallet and passport were still there, clean and dry. Jack dropped them into his extra-safe pocket – the one with a loop and a string to tie it shut – and walked out of the hut.

~

'DO YOU KNOW Alex Rover?' Nim asked Erin, when Ben had gone to buy an ice-cream, because some things are easier to say to one person than two.

'Alex Rover the famous writer?'

'She's my friend,' said Nim. 'And my dad's friend. But I was mean to her, and mean to my dad, and now she's gone.'

'Everybody's mean sometimes,' said Erin, though Nim knew Erin could never be as mean as she had been.

'My dad will be worrying that she'll never come back,' said Nim, 'and he might be worried about me, too. Or…he might be glad I'm gone.'

'He won't be glad you're gone,' said Erin.

'I wish I could tell him where I am,' said Nim.

'You could email him from the computer room.'

'Parents have to log their kids in,' said Ben, handing them each an ice-cream cone.

'Write down the message and the address,' said Erin, 'and I'll send it.'

'Thanks,' said Nim. 'Whew! I never knew ice-cream was so cold!

From: erin@kidmail.com
To: jack.rusoe@explorer.net
Date: Friday 2 July, 11:05am
Subject: Don't worry!

Dear Jack

My friend Erin is sending this because I can't go to the Computer Room unless you sign me in.

I hope you got my message in a bottle. I'm on the Troppo Tourist ship heading towards New York.

We have a plan but I don't want to write it down in case someone sees the note when Erin is writing it.

I cleaned out the birdcages this morning and four flaming orange doves had our island's bands on their legs. I didn't know people were allowed to catch animals just because they're intelligent, unique or interesting. The Professor says that's the best way to keep them safe. I don't understand but he doesn't like people asking questions.

Also I don't think he really like animals.

I'm very very sorry I was mean to Alex and I know I was mean to you sometimes when you were talking to Alex. I wish I hadn't been.

Love (as much as Fred loves Selkie)

Nim

She wrote one to Alex too, but in the end she couldn't bear Erin to read it, so she crumpled it up and put it back in her pocket.

~

'IT'S PIZZA NIGHT in the Kids' Klub,' Ben said, while Erin was emailing, 'so we can all have dinner there.'

'What's pizza like?' asked Nim.

Ben explained. 'But you can't ask anyone but us stuff like that! They'll guess...'

'They'll guess I'm a stowaway?'

'They'll probably just think you're weird,' said Ben, 'and that'll make them notice you. Even more than Fred.'

So when Erin came back they found a spot behind a big white chest labelled LIFE JACKETS, up near the bow where it was too windy for most people to sit, and Nim got lessons on how to look as if she belonged to parents on a cruise ship.

It was sort of like schoolwork with Jack, except that instead of learning about what turtles ate and how plankton grew, she was learning about what kids ate and what they said; what they did and what they had.

'There's so much stuff!' Nim groaned. 'And so much to learn! How am I going to remember it all?'

'Stick with us,' said Erin. 'Just do what we do.'

As Ben looked at his watch, Nim looked up at the sun. 'But first,' she said, 'it's time for Fred and me to visit Selkie.'

Chapter 9

SELKIE AND FRED both knew lots of tricks, but they only did them when they wanted to. It was hard for Nim to make them understand that the only way they were going to outsmart the Professor was to do the tricks Nim wanted, when she asked.

And the Professor was watching. He was in a very bad mood because one of the baby spider monkeys had bitten him while he was giving his lecture.

Nim didn't want him to be angry at Selkie, too, so first she fed the birds, chirping quietly to them in their own languages.

'If you make bird noises, they'll never learn to talk!' the Professor snapped. 'Teach them "Pretty Polly!" That's what people pay…are interested in.'

Without waiting for an answer, he stomped out the door. Nim was alone with the animals.

She clucked to the doves once more and rushed to open Selkie's cage. Selkie whuffled and sniffed her all over, as if Nim was the one who'd been seal-napped and locked up.

'We'll get home somehow,' Nim told her. 'Because even

if Alex doesn't like me any more, I know she'll help us get back.'

'Anyway,' she added, 'the important thing is to escape. We've got five days to get ready.'

She looked at Selkie's little cage and the cloudy tub of water, and five days seemed for ever.

'If I could just get you into a pool,' she said, 'it wouldn't be so bad.'

Very quietly, she turned the door handle. It wasn't locked. She opened it a crack and peered down the hall.

The Professor was coming.

Nim shut the door quickly. She hugged Selkie hard and just for a minute she thought she was going to cry – but that would upset Selkie more than being in a cage.

And it was crying that got us into this mess in the first place! Nim thought, which suddenly seemed so silly she almost laughed – except now the Professor was in the room again, so instead she clapped.

'Fantastic!' she said, as if Selkie had just done the most wonderful trick in the world.

Then she added quickly, in case the Professor asked to see it, 'That's enough training for today.'

The Professor grunted. 'Okay, kid, get the rest of those animals fed and cleaned out. If you do a good job I'll let you do some more training in the morning.'

'Thank you,' Nim said politely, working as slowly and carefully as she could, because every minute she was here was a minute Selkie wasn't locked in her cage alone.

Suddenly, she spotted a key hanging behind the door. It looked just like the Professor's, but she'd seen him drop his into his pocket. This one had to be a spare – and if it was a spare, he might not notice if it was missing.

So Nim brushed the rotten fruit and droppings out of the monkeys' cage, put in clean water and not-quite-rotten fruit and murmured quietly to them, trying not to let them feel how sad and angry she was to see them there.

Finally she put Selkie back in her cage, sitting beside her for a long moment to rub her head with love and cool water.

'Just remember,' the Professor said, with his sneering smile, 'this place is our little secret. The Foundation's work is very important – much too important for most people to understand. I don't ever want to hear you talking about the animals down here.

'So, my little stowaway friend, just keep your mouth shut and everyone will be happy: I'll get a fat stack of money, the animals will get lovely new homes that appreciate how intelligent, unique and interesting they are – and you and your mum can stay out of jail.'

Nim swallowed hard, and nodded. He wanted her to be afraid, and she was. More afraid than she'd ever been. She was so afraid that the Professor knew he didn't have to worry about her at all. He sat calmly down in his chair in the corner, opened a can of drink and started to read his newspaper.

'I'll come back in the morning,' Nim whispered.

The Professor grunted and turned a page.

Nim backed to the door – and as she waved goodbye to Selkie, snatched the key off its hook.

Chapter 10

THE HARDEST THING about fitting in at Pizza Night, Nim decided, was acting as if the biggest problem in her life was getting a piece with pepperoni when she wanted anchovies (because at least anchovies were fish and tasted a bit like home).

'It's like swimming with a new pod of dolphins,' she told Ben and Erin, when they took their pizzas out to the deck to sit alone.

'I wish I could do that!' Ben exclaimed.

'I wish we could go to your island,' Erin said.

'I wish you could, too,' said Nim. Saying it made her feel hot inside, as if she were betraying Jack – but it was true. She used to wonder what it would be like to have friends that could talk. Now she'd found out, and she liked it. Nim wanted to be back on her island more than anything else, but she didn't want to lose Erin and Ben.

She told them what the Professor had said.

'Jail!' repeated Erin.

'But he's the bad guy!' Ben said fiercely.

'He says he's allowed to catch the animals, because of

191

this Foundation. He says that's the law, because catching them educates people and protects other animals all around the world.'

'And he *is* a Professor,' said Erin.

'And I *am* a stowaway,' said Nim.

'But he's still bad,' said Ben.

'We should ask Mum and Dad,' said Erin.

'No!' shouted Nim. 'He said he'd send me to the Captain if I ever told anyone. I shouldn't even have told you – and if you help me you'll get into trouble too!'

'We don't care,' Ben said.

'All that matters,' Erin agreed, 'is keeping you safe and getting Selkie free. So we just have to stick to our plan.'

'But the best thing we can do right now,' said Ben, 'is try to look like we're having a good time. Let's get some more pizza!'

Fred rubbed his spiny back against Ben's leg. Fred had mozzarella strings tangled from his grinning mouth to his claws. He liked pizza, and he liked Ben more and more.

～

NIM FELT LONELY, climbing back up into her lifeboat with Fred while Erin and Ben stood watch outside their cabin door.

It felt lonely, and when she'd pulled the cover over, it felt dark – black as the deepest sea.

Then she heard a knock – the three quick knocks and two slow that were their signal – then the rocking of someone climbing the struts.

Ben stuck his head in to hand her a torch.

Nim turned it on, and saw why Erin had looked as if she was going to burst with her own secret when she'd said, 'Sleep tight, Nim!'

The boat had been turned into a bedroom. There were two blankets to sleep on, two towels for covers, a pillow for her and one for Fred, a bottle of water and a banana.

But best of all was remembering the look on Erin and Ben's faces when she'd shown them the key to Selkie's prison. They'd touched it as if it were magic – and even though Nim wasn't a magician, just knowing it was in her pocket made her almost as powerful.

～

IT WAS SO early the sun wasn't up when Erin rapped three 'wake up!' knocks on the metal strut.

Still half asleep, Nim dropped her pillows and blankets over the side to Erin, just in case a Troppo Tourist used the boat during the day. Then she swung down to the deck, with Fred following. The cool morning air woke them quickly. While Erin tiptoed back into her cabin to hide the bedding, Nim and Fred raced down to the Animal Room. When there was no one around to step on him, Fred liked walking.

With a quick check that no one was watching, Nim unlocked the door and they slipped inside.

'Hurry!' she whispered to Selkie as she undid the cage. She felt sorry for the others, but she couldn't help them yet.

Selkie galumphed down the hall after her and into the elevator, honking with surprise when it went up. Fred grinned a little wider, as if he'd been doing this since he was hatched.

It was dark and deserted as they came out onto the Sea Lion Deck. They raced to the Waterslide Pool and dived into the clear water.

Selkie snorted and rolled, dived and leapt, around and around the pool as fast as she could. Fred sank to the bottom and came up again, sneezing with disgust because he couldn't find any seaweed.

Nim swam with Selkie and dived with Fred; she couldn't swim as fast as a sea lion or hold her breath as long as a marine iguana, but she liked trying. She didn't know exactly how they were going to escape, but she did know they'd all need to be as strong, as fast, and as good at everything as they could possibly be.

The sky began to pale. A man hurried past, buttoning his white chef's jacket.

Nim signed to Selkie, and Selkie dived as silently as a whisper. Fred was already down at the bottom again; he was sure there must be seaweed somewhere. Nim kept on swimming and tried not to splash.

'You're up early!' the chef called. 'Trying to beat the rush?'

'Yes,' said Nim, and he hurried on by.

Nim knew it was too dangerous to stay any longer. They slipped out and back to the hold, with nothing but a quickly drying trail of water to tell where they'd been.

Chapter 11

JACK WOKE UP with the sun. He'd steered all night, with a few quick naps in between. Now the daylight showed him that he still had a long, long way to go – there was no sign of land in all this wide blue sea.

A frigate bird circled low to see if he had any fish. 'Nothing today, Galileo!' Jack called. He wished he could tuck a note into the big bird's leg band, but even Galileo couldn't find Nim in a city.

For just a minute Jack wondered what he'd do if Nim wasn't with Alex – but he pushed that thought away.

As Galileo disappeared into the sky, Jack shouted, 'You're right, I should put those lines out now! Thanks for reminding me!'

He checked his compass, pointed the sail to head four points further east, threw his fishing lines in, and had a drink of water and some coconut for breakfast.

'I'll be with you soon, Nim!' he called.

Then he added more quietly, 'And you too, Alex. I hope.'

~

ALEX WOKE WITH a start. She was sure someone had

knocked on her cabin door: three quick raps. Then there was a thump of someone jumping onto the deck, and whispering.

It was just the children from the cabin next door. She'd heard them during the day; it sounded as if there were two very little girls, a boy and another girl about Nim's age, and maybe even another girl. She could never hear what they said, just the buzz of their voices and thumps from their cabin when they jumped to the floor or dumped things out of cupboards.

Alex wondered what they were like. She wondered if they'd know how to be friends with Nim. Maybe I'd have been better at it if I'd met other kids before I went to the island, she thought.

'Because if you'd been better at it,' she told herself, 'you wouldn't be on this ship right now!'

'And don't you dare cry again!' she added, and made herself go back to sleep.

~

NIM HAD GOT Selkie back just in time. It was now bright, busy daylight, and people were swarming everywhere, settling into deck chairs and crowding the rails. One of them would have probably noticed a sea lion galumphing through the ship.

It was busy out on the water, too: there were more ships ahead, behind, and coming towards them. They were going down a wide river with bright green hills close on either side, and Nim felt tight and closed-in when she could suddenly

196

see only a narrow strip of water instead of the wide blue sea she was used to.

The river became skinnier and the banks grew steeper, until it was such a narrow canal that their ship was nearly touching both concrete sides. Very gently, they were tugged up to a pair of locked giant doors. Another pair of doors shut behind them – and just as Nim was wondering where the ship could go next, it started going up as if it were in an elevator.

Nim tried to look as if she were used to being on ships that went up and down elevators, until she saw that nearly everyone on board had come out to watch and take pictures.

'Amazing!'

'How does it work?'

'The water comes in through culverts from a lake.'

'I've wanted to see this all my life!'

But everything's strange to me! thought Nim. How am I supposed to know which ones are strange to everyone else?

She saw Erin and Ben, with their parents and little sisters, watching from outside their cabin while their mother videoed the giant elevator doors.

Now the dock on the other side of the railing was the same height as the deck. If she jumped over the railing right now she could probably escape the ship.

'But we can't leave without Selkie,' she whispered to Fred. Fred rubbed his head under her chin.

The ship went up higher and higher till they were way too far above the dock to jump.

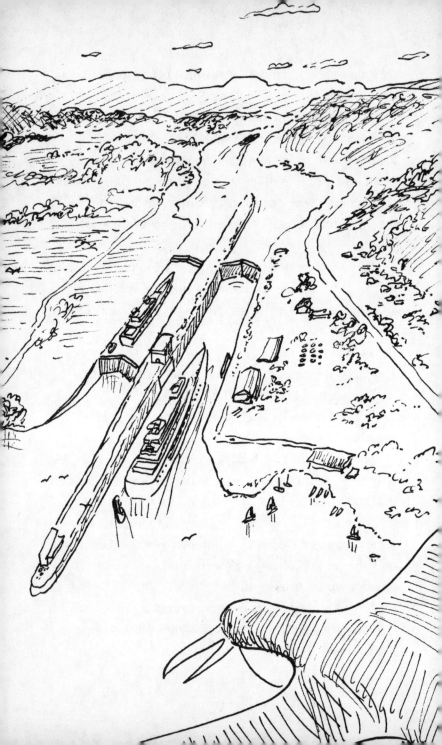

Anyway, thought Nim, if we'd got off here, how would I ever find Alex?

And how would I ever find home?

Maybe we'll have to stay on the ship for ever, and never go ashore again.

~

THAT AFTERNOON IN the Kids' Klub, Kelvin taught them to play Spiderweb. The person who was Spider stood in the middle with their hands above their head, while all the other kids squashed up in a circle around them. When Kelvin shouted 'Web!' they had to reach behind, grab the first two hands they met, and keep on holding them while they all wiggled around, forward and back, to get back into a circle – while the Spider tried to get through to the other side.

'But no hitting or kicking!' Kristie warned. 'Spiders don't hurt their own net!'

Nim was good at being Spider, because she could squirm under arms or slither through legs faster than anyone. But what she liked best was holding tight to Erin or Ben or kids she didn't know, and just being part of the web.

From: erin@kidmail.com
To: jack.rusoe@explorer.net
Date: Saturday 3 July, 5:45pm
Subject: More information

Dear Jack

I thought you might have answered by now but I guess you are very busy since I'm not there to help you with the science stuff.

Today the Professor took pictures of me holding the birds and cage animals. He says the Foundation likes to see pictures like this to show how intelligent, unique and interesting the animals are, to prove why they should be protected. He dressed one of the spider monkeys up like a baby and I thought it looked silly and it couldn't have swung around even if it wasn't in a cage, but I played a swinging game with it afterwards to cheer it up.

Selkie is a lot happier today because she had a swim in the pool and Fred was happy because he tasted pizza last night and today Ben brought him a whole pocketful of salad for lunch. I've had lots of different food, too. Ben and Erin said I shouldn't ask for a seaweed sandwich because people would think that was strange and they might guess I'm a stowaway. It's quite funny because when you want food here you don't have to make it or catch it yourself.

I saw a frigate bird today. I wished it was Galileo with a message from you.

Love (as much as Galileo loves stealing fish)
Nim

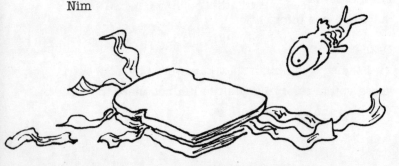

Chapter 12

'I'VE GOT AN idea,' Nim said, the morning after the ship went through the elevator canal, because the Professor was whistling a cheerful whistle, and she needed him to be in a good mood so she could start putting their plan into action. 'You know how you give a lecture about animals every day? When you do the sea lion lecture on Wednesday, it could be like a show – like a circus! And I could help.'

'There's not enough time. I know all there is to know about training animals – it takes months for them to learn to do tricks on command.'

'But this sea lion is amazingly smart – and so is the iguana. I bet I could get them ready for you, especially if I could train them in a pool.'

'That beast will go to the Sea Lion Pool,' snarled the Professor, 'when I'm sure she won't bite anyone else.'

I wish she'd bitten you harder! Nim thought. 'She was probably just scared,' she said. 'I'm positive she won't do it again.'

'She'd better not,' said the Professor, glancing at his whip.

'Everyone could see how intelligent, unique and interesting they both are.'

'Well, maybe we can do a show on Wednesday morning. Then if she behaves, she can stay in the Sea Lion Pool till she's sold…till she's relocated.'

Relocated? thought Nim, feeling as if she'd just swallowed a bucket of cold water. How would I ever get her back then?

But we won't let that happen! she reminded herself fiercely. We've still got three days to get our show ready – and then we'll escape.

'You can have a couple of hours in the afternoons to practise. And…' the Professor paused and stared at her as if he knew exactly what she was thinking, 'it had better be good.'

~

'BUT HOW'S IT going to be good if we can't use the big pool?' Nim demanded, when she and Erin and Ben were in the Kids' Klub carving watermelons into interesting sculptures. Kristie had demonstrated how to carve a Viking's head and a sailboat, and now each kid had a watermelon and a blunt knife, and could carve whatever they liked.

Nim used her own sharp pocketknife to carve Selkie. Erin carved a cat, and Ben made a Viking's head that was nearly as good as Kristie's.

Fred ate the whole middle out of a watermelon and made an empty rowboat. Everyone clapped, and he scrambled back onto Nim's shoulder, looking smug.

'Do you think that could be a trick?' Nim asked.

'I don't think so,' said Erin. 'But I *have* figured out how you can use the Waterslide pool for your show.'

～

JACK HAD BEEN on his raft for three days. He still had two coconuts and half a container of water, but he was a bit sore, very stiff, and very, very tired. It was not a big raft and it was not comfortable at all.

There was a line on the horizon that could have been cloud or…Sunshine Island? Jack hoped so.

The closer he sailed the clearer and less cloudlike the line became. By noon he was sure. It was definitely land. Jack tightened the sail and whistled for wind.

A speck of light caught his eye. A bottle was bobbing on the waves – with something inside it.

If Nim had been with him, they would have chased and grabbed it.

But they'd never ever found a message – and if Nim had been with him he wouldn't be going to Sunshine Island on a raft made out of the wall of their hut. Jack let the bottle float by, and sailed on as fast as he could.

~

ALEX HAD SPENT three whole days alone in her cabin. She hadn't spoken to anyone except Virginia the steward, when she brought her juice every morning, and came back a little later to clean. 'What a shame you're not feeling better!' Virginia said. 'You'd have so much fun if you could get out there and meet people.' But Alex had left behind the only people she wanted to know.

She even kept her curtains closed, because all she could see was people walking by, and the lifeboat stands, which weren't very interesting.

And, even though there were pens and writing paper in her cabin's desk, she hadn't written a word. For the first time in her life, there was no story in her head.

Worst of all, she didn't care.

From: erin@kidmail.com
To: jack.rusoe@explorer.net
Date: Sunday 4 July, 5:30pm
Subject: Important!

Dear Jack

Selkie and Fred and I are going to put on a show, so we practised for two hours this afternoon. It's horrible being with Selkie when the Professor's watching because I have to pretend I don't know her, and pretend I'm training her to do tricks, even though it's just the games we play at home. But Selkie thinks it's better than being in the cage so she doesn't mind pretending. Fred hates the Professor so much he just glares at him all the time but the Professor never notices.

It's very interesting being on the ship but I still like our island better. I hope you will stop being mad at me soon.

Love (as much as Jack loves the island)
Nim

'No message yet,' Erin said to Nim, when she came back from sending Nim's email to Jack. She tried to sound as if it wasn't important, as if she didn't know that Nim was worrying whether Jack was too angry to answer or if there was another reason that was even worse.

'Maybe he keeps forgetting to charge the battery,' Nim said.

'Probably,' said Erin.

'Or a virus!' said Ben.

'Maybe,' said Nim.

'We've got an hour before dinner,' said Ben. 'Let's play Spy.'

'Dolphin Deck?' asked Erin.

'Butterfly,' said Nim, and started up the stairs. She always went first when they played Spy, because it was harder for someone with an iguana on their shoulder to blend into a crowd.

She chose the Butterfly Deck because the butterflies were the only animals on the ship that didn't make her feel sad. They had plenty of space to fly around, and she loved it when they landed on her hair and arms. Nim wandered slowly through the butterfly cage, with Fred sitting so still, that her head and Fred's spine were soon covered with brightly coloured butterflies. They both smiled so much that even the happy kissy people, who came in from the wedding room to have their pictures taken, didn't notice that she didn't belong in their party.

Chapter 13

FROM ONE END of Sunshine Island to the other, people stared as Jack sailed his raft past the roaring jet skis, through the swimmers and snorkellers in the calm water, and right up onto the beach between the sunbathers and sandcastles.

He pulled down the sail and folded it into its bag, in case he needed it again. Curious people gathered around.

'Where's the airport?' Jack asked.

Someone pointed down the road.

Someone else took his picture.

'It's a long walk,' one man said. 'I'll drive you.'

Jack followed him to a golf buggy parked at the top of the beach, and the crowd drifted back to their sunbathing and sandcastles.

But when they reached the airport: 'You're in luck!' said the man at the airport ticket counter. 'You can get on a flight tomorrow morning.'

'I need to go today!' said Jack.

'Tuesdays and Thursdays – that's it.'

Thursday! thought Jack. That's the day Alex and Nim left. If they missed the flight, they'll still be here.

The man with the golf buggy drove him all around the town till late at night, but they never found a sign of Alex or Nim.

~

'YOU,' SAID ALEX to herself as she sat cross-legged on her bunk to eat her dinner, 'are a lazy lay-a-bed slobby slug. You've gone through the Panama Canal without even seeing it. What if you need a story Hero to stow away on a ship on a great ocean adventure – how are you going to write about it?

'Same way I always do,' she answered. 'Reading, research and imagination.'

'Except the last book,' said Alex, 'you lived that one. That's why it's your best story – and the best part of your life.'

But she hadn't been brave enough to open it yet.

~

KIDS' KLUB FINISHED at five o'clock, but a big bunch of kids were out on the Sea Lion deck when Erin, Nim and Ben wandered up there after dinner. Nim had just finished eating her smuggled food when a small pig-tailed girl tapped Ben on the shoulder. 'Spider!' she shouted.

Quick as a wink, everyone else grabbed the nearest hands to make the web; Ben wriggled and squirmed to get through and the others held tight until the small pig-tailed girl began to giggle and they all collapsed together in a wiggling, giggling heap, happy as a pile of sea lion pups in the sun.

~

LATER THAT NIGHT, with her windows open to catch the breeze, Alex heard the next-door parents chatting on the deck after their children had gone to bed. She imagined them leaning over the rail to watch the moonlight dancing on the waves.

'The kids seem to be having a good time,' the father was saying. 'They've made lots of new friends.'

'And they're certainly enjoying the food! They keep heaping their plates with more than they could possibly eat, but when I look again, it's gone.'

'This fresh sea air's certainly giving them an appetite,' the father agreed.

Chapter 14

THE NEXT MORNING, Nim, Selkie and Fred snuck up even earlier to swim in the Waterslide Pool. With the three of them all together, they felt almost free.

At the first sounds of the crew bustling around, they scurried back to Selkie's prison. A few moments later, the ship dropped anchor in a white sand harbour.

Nim locked Selkie in and ran upstairs to say good morning to the dolphins in the fountain. When she went back to the Animal Room, the Professor was waiting for her to start feeding and cleaning.

'No time for that!' he snapped, when Nim hugged Selkie. 'Feed them and get out. I don't want you around today.'

'But you said I could practise this afternoon!'

'I've changed my mind. Now snap to it and then scram!'

His eyes were narrow, his face was hard – and he kept glancing at his whip. Nim fed the animals, and got out.

~

'EVERYONE'S GOING ASHORE,' Erin told Nim. 'I wish you could come, but they check the tickets extra carefully when people get back on. It wouldn't be safe.'

'They'll probably use your inflatable,' Ben added. 'Did you get all your things?'

Nim nodded. Everything was tucked safely into Erin's wardrobe.

'The Kids' Klub is shut too,' Erin said sadly, 'so you'd better stay in our cabin.'

Nim had to wander up and down the deck while Erin and Ben's mother hurried in and out of the cabins to organise their day. She felt as empty as a pricked balloon when Ben and Erin finally disappeared down the stairs with their family.

A second later, Erin came running back down the hall.

'I said I forgot my hat,' she puffed, unlocking the cabin door. 'There are some books on my bed, if you want to read, and television, and paper and textas for making the posters. I *wish* you could come!'

Erin grabbed her hat, shouted, 'Bye!' and ran out. Nim started looking through the books. One was *Mountain Madness*, by Alex Rover. Nim remembered when she first read it, when she was alone on the island and Alex had emailed to ask Jack about coconuts. Alex had tried to tell Nim she wasn't really the Hero of her story, but Nim hadn't believed her. She wondered if she would still like the book now she knew Alex was just a small scared woman who'd sailed across the world to help Nim, before she even knew her.

She lay on Erin's bed and started reading.

There was a knock, and Ben bounced in. 'We forgot to tell you – breakfast is in the desk!'

He raced out again, and Nim found a brown-bread sandwich and an apple in the drawer.

Fred didn't like brown bread, and he didn't like apples, but he was hungry enough to share. 'We'll find you something,' Nim said, though she wasn't sure what.

They had a shower; Nim changed into the clothes Erin had left for her, and sat down at the desk with the papers and coloured pens. She drew twenty-two SEA LION CIRCUS posters – two for each passenger deck – exactly how she'd planned them with Erin and Ben. When she'd finished, she tucked them neatly into the desk drawer, flopped back onto Erin's bed, and went on reading.

Rap! Tap!

Someone was knocking at the door.

Nim stayed very still and didn't answer. Fred crept behind a lamp and went to sleep.

The door opened, and a steward in a white uniform and blue apron came in with a vacuum cleaner and a mop and bucket. She saw Nim, and dropped her bucket.

'Yipes!' Virginia squeaked. 'Did your parents leave you here alone?'

Nim nodded, because she couldn't tell the truth.

'Are you sick?'

Nim nodded again.

Virginia shook her head sympathetically. 'Sorry – I still have to clean,' she said, 'but I'll be as quiet as I can.'

She straightened Ben's bed and made Nim sit on it while she changed Erin's. 'Leaving a sick child alone!' Nim heard her muttering. 'Appalling!'

Nim thought about Erin and Ben's parents, and her face grew as hot and red as the lava in Fire Mountain. 'I'm feeling a lot better now!'

Virginia finished cleaning, felt Nim's forehead and made her go back to bed.

Nim picked up *Mountain Madness* again. She read lying down, she read sitting up, and she read lying on the floor with her feet on the bed. Then she practised doing handstands, and Fred practised climbing from her shoulder to her feet instead of the usual way around. They even made up a trick with Fred staying stiff as a log and Nim twirling him around on her feet.

But you can't stay upside down spinning an iguana for ever, so after that Nim stared out through the lifeboat stands at a bit of blue sea. A great black frigate bird soared past. Looking through her spyglass she was almost sure it was Galileo. 'I wish I could go out on deck to check,' she muttered, even though she didn't have a fish to call him with.

One more chapter of *Mountain Madness*; the hero had just caught a trout in a mountain stream and cooked it over a fire.

'I should have saved the apple for lunch,' Nim told Fred. Fred answered with his best unblinking stare. He was sure she could find them some food if she tried hard enough.

'We can't go out,' she told him, 'because everyone else has gone ashore, and the crew will notice me and ask where my parents are.'

There was another knock at the door. Nim shoved a pillow over Fred, and Virginia tiptoed in carrying a tray.

'I wasn't sure what you liked,' she said, 'so I brought sandwiches and salad, fruit, cake…'

The pillow wiggled. Nim put her elbow on it. 'Thank you. That's very nice of you.'

She was glad she could say something that wasn't a lie.

'I'm so pleased you're starting to feel better. The poor lady next door hasn't left her cabin for the whole trip!'

This cabin was a bright room with cheerful paintings on the walls, but Nim thought she'd have gone crazy if she'd spent the whole trip in it.

'You look a bit bored,' Virginia said, as she left. 'Do you want the TV on?' She handed Nim the remote control.

'Thanks,' said Nim.

But even though Nim had seen televisions in the lounges when they played Spy, and she'd played video games in the Kids' Klub, she'd never sat and watched a program with a story – and she'd never had the remote. Neither had Fred. Fred didn't care about the programs, but he liked stepping on the buttons so that the channel changed just as Nim figured out what was happening.

'Stop it, Fred!' Nim shouted.

Fred went to sulk under the bed, and Nim turned the TV off. She didn't want to shout again and wake up that poor sick lady next door.

'Come on…you can have all the lettuce,' she coaxed, and when Fred had eaten the lettuce out of the sandwich and sneezed a kiwi fruit all over the bed, he felt quite cheerful again.

Nim finished *Mountain Madness* and stared out the window some more.

When she heard the rumble of the launches and the thump of passengers' feet on the gangplank, she grabbed Fred and raced outside to gulp deep breaths of fresh air.

And as soon as the ship was on its way out to sea again, Nim pulled on her Troppo Tourist jacket and ran down the stairs to the Animal Room. She waited outside the door until the Professor let her in.

Selkie whuffled sadly, because it had been an even longer day for her. And scarier.

The last of the empty cages was full now – with long, fat snakes.

From: erin@kidmail.com
To: jack.rusoe@explorer.net
Date: Monday 5 July, 7:30pm
Subject: Very important!

Dear Jack

Maybe there's something wrong with the computer and that's why you're not answering, but I think you'd want to know what we're doing so I'll go on emailing and maybe you can read it later.

Today I had to stay inside the cabin all day and it was very boring but now I understand even better how Selkie must be feeling, and all the other animals with her. So maybe it was good in some ways.

Erin bought me a bead bracelet when she went ashore. It's very pretty and she bought one for herself just the same so whenever we wear them we will think about each other. Ben brought Fred and me a coconut, which was good because we haven't had coconut for way too long.

Love (as much as Fred loves coconut)

Nim

Chapter 15

JACK SPENT THE night on the floor of his new friend's living room.

'Who are you?' the man joked, when he saw Jack staring at the television as if he couldn't remember what it was. 'Robinson Crusoe?'

'No – Jack Rusoe.'

His friend laughed, but Jack couldn't. He'd just checked his emails – and not one message had come into the Inbox. Only the Trash folder had blinked as the Spam trickled in to be deleted.

The next morning he sorted out how to get money at the bank, and took the little plane to the airport on Isla Grande.

The only thing he could do now was to go and see Delia Defoe. She wasn't just Alex's editor – she was probably the only person in the world who knew where Alex was.

There was one seat left on the plane leaving the next day for New York City.

~

'THERE'S A SEA lion circus tomorrow,' Virginia told Alex when she brought in her breakfast. 'There are posters all over the ship – doesn't that sound fun?'

If Alex hadn't known Selkie she might have thought it sounded fun. But she did know Selkie, and suddenly she missed her so much that she knew she could never see another sea lion again without crying. It was the best reason so far for staying in her cabin another day.

~

ERIN WOKE NIM and Fred up earlier than usual, but they spent so long in the pool that the sun had come up before they knew it. When Nim came up for air after practising swimming underwater, a white-uniformed crewman was standing at the edge, watching.

'There's a sea lion in there!' he exclaimed.

'It's the Sea Lion Deck,' said Nim.

'But this is a swimming pool. For people.'

'We need it to practise for the sea lion circus,' said Nim. 'We won't need it after tomorrow.'

'The cruise ends tomorrow!'

'That's why we won't need it,' said Nim.

The crewman stared a little longer, then shrugged and walked away.

Nim and her friends scrambled out of the pool and back to the Animal Room, as fast as they could.

~

'I SUPPOSE YOU think you're clever!' the Professor snarled when he let Nim in to feed the animals. 'All those posters advertising a sea lion circus at the Waterslide Pool – now you think I'll have to let that beast in there!'

'I must have got mixed up!' said Nim, even though the posters were exactly how she wanted them. 'Isn't that what you meant?'

'I said you could have her perform a few tricks at my lecture. You know perfectly well it was supposed to be in the theatre, like all my lectures. I'm a professor – that's what people expect.'

'I just thought…'

'Think about what's going to happen to you and your mum if you try to be smart. Besides, no one's going to look at humdrum animal tricks once we get into the harbour. You'd better do something spectacular or you won't have an audience.'

'I've got a plan,' said Nim. 'It'll be spectacualar.'

~

'THE POSTERS WORKED!' Nim said, as Erin handed her a breakfast scrambled-egg sandwich, and Ben tossed grapes for Fred to catch. 'We can do the show the way we planned.'

'So today…'

'We can do whatever we like.'

It was hard to choose, because even though in some ways today was exactly like every other day on the ship, it was the last day they were going to spend together, and that made it special – sad, and a little bit scary.

Fred chose to spend the day at the Splash Pool, where

he could sit on the water jets and be blasted into the air and then paddle across the pool, just the way he liked to do where the spray came in at a blowhole at the Black Rocks.

Ben, Erin and Nim went on a treasure hunt with the other kids from the Kids' Klub. The clues took them all over the ship, but when Nim got to the Toucan Deck she found the toucan sitting on the floor of its cage with its head drooping and eyes closed.

Nim squatted down to see it. It's so unhappy it might die! she thought. Suddenly she knew that escaping with Selkie was not enough. Every animal on the ship had to be rescued.

'Just hang in there a little bit longer! We're going to help you, somehow,' Nim told the unhappy bird, chirping and clucking until it lifted its head to see her. When it finally began to peck its mushed mango, Nim stood up – and noticed the treasure chest hidden behind the display. It was full of enough bags of candy for everyone in the Kids' Klub.

Fred thought he liked candy, but he felt sick afterwards and had to lie on his back while Nim rubbed his tummy.

Then Nim and Erin painted all the papier mâché fish they'd been making, and Ben finished his sculpture.

'Excellent!' said Kristie.

'It *is* pretty good,' Erin admitted.

'It's amazing,' said Nim.

But Fred hated it, because it looked exactly like him. He walked all around it, glaring, and then climbed up to Nim's shoulder to glare some more.

'It's so I'll remember you when you're not around,' Ben explained.

Fred blinked, but Nim thought she might cry.

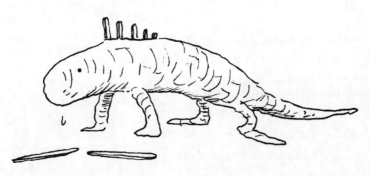

LATER IN THE afternoon, down in the prison, Selkie and Nim practised handstands, and Fred practised spinning on Selkie's flippers. It wasn't the most important trick, but it was the start of something bigger.

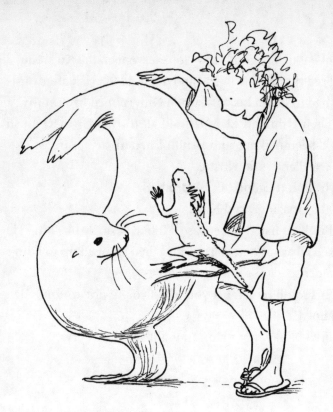

'Sleep tight,' Nim whispered to Selkie when it was time to leave. 'Everything happens tomorrow.'

From: erin@kidmail.com
To: jack.rusoe@explorer.net
Date: Tuesday 6 July, 5:36pm
Subject: You must read this!

Dear Jack

I haven't had an email from Alex yet either so if she is still angry at me too this might be the last email I can write to you. I don't know what I'm going to do but I can't worry about it because first we have to get off the ship. Sometimes I wish you could sail up to the ship and rescue us, but you don't have a boat any more so I know you couldn't do that even if you weren't angry at me.

The Professor made me cut the bands off the island doves' legs today. But if our plans go right it won't matter. Also I've made notes in my notebook about the birds' markings so we can identify them again. I've made notes about all the animals on the ship because I thought you would want me to do that.

A frigate bird has been following the ship for the last three days. It's been flying too high for me to be sure but I think it really is Galileo.

I hope I'll see you and our island again soon.

Love (as much as Selkie loves diving)

Nim

There was a special Kids' Klub dinner for the last night of the cruise so, for the first time, Nim ate in the dining room with her friends. She borrowed a skirt and top from Erin, and brushed her wild hair till it was nearly neat. Fred was sleepy, so he crawled under Ben's bed to rest.

'Are you sure you don't want to come?' Nim asked, but Fred just blinked and went back to sleep.

Her shoulders felt light and empty without him, but it made blending in easier.

Which was important because, after the dinner with the

other Klub Kids, Nim was going to spend the night in Ben and Erin's cabin.

'Your dad doesn't mind you sleeping over?' their mum asked.

'No,' said Nim, because it didn't seem as if Jack minded about her at all, and if he did, he'd probably rather she slept in a cabin than on the floor of a lifeboat.

Erin loaned her some pyjamas and they squashed into the bed together. Fred stayed under Ben's bed. Nim didn't know if it was to say goodbye to Ben, or because he was just too sound asleep to move.

They talked and talked in the darkness. None of them wanted to think about tomorrow but there was still plenty to talk about till Mr and Mrs Caritas came in to say goodnight.

~

'DON'T TALK TOO late,' Mr Caritas said. 'It's a big day tomorrow. Do you live in New York, Nim?'

'No,' said Nim. 'It's my first visit.'

'You'll love it! But for us the holiday's over: We'll be going straight to the airport to fly home.'

Their mum bent to kiss Erin on the forehead, and then she kissed Nim too. It felt just like when Alex used to kiss her goodnight.

Alex! Nim thought into the night, but even in her head she couldn't quite sort out all the things she wanted to say, so she sent the wish out in a big jumble of love, sorriness and hope.

Ben's voice trickled off into soft snores, but Erin and Nim whispered still.

The door opened quietly. 'You really have to go to sleep now,' said Erin's mum, 'or Nim will have to go back to her dad.'

'That's what you're trying to do!' Erin whispered when the door closed again, and they started to giggle. They giggled so hard they had to put the pillows over their heads, and then Erin went to sleep.

~

ALEX HEARD NIM calling – and then she heard her giggle. She was wide awake and at the door before she realised she must have been dreaming again.

But it seemed so real! she thought.

Nim! she thought into the night, but even in her head she couldn't quite sort out all the things she wanted to say, so she sent the wish out in a big jumble of love, sorriness and hope.

~

NIM STOPPED WORRYING and wondering, and fell fast asleep.

Chapter 16

NIM HUGGED ERIN and Ben goodbye. They'd see each other later, but they wouldn't be able to talk. She gave Ben her green stone and Erin the bamboo cup that had been in her pockets when she jumped off the cliff. Finally she gave Ben the bird bands, the Troppo Tourist jacket and most important of all, the key.

Then she dressed in her own clothes – her bright blue shirt and baggy red pants with drawstring ties and useful pockets – and went down to the Animal Room. She gave the cage animals love and breakfast, trying to let them feel her hope: 'You'll be free soon!'

By nine o'clock there were more butterflies in her stomach than on the Butterfly Deck. It was time for the circus.

The Professor picked up his whip.

'You don't need the whip,' Nim said bravely. 'Grownups won't like it and it will scare the kids.'

The Professor flicked a warning crack. 'Then you'd better keep those animals under control – because I'll be keeping it close at hand, just in case.'

Nim shut her mouth so hard her teeth hurt. It was the only way she could stop herself from shouting every bad name she'd ever heard. She opened the door.

'Selkie, walk!' she ordered. 'Fred, follow!'

'Sorry,' she whispered, as they started down the hall. 'After today, I'll *never* talk to you like that again!'

Selkie looked at her with her head on one side and Nim knew she understood, but Fred scuttled along behind looking as cross as an iguana can possibly look.

It was a tight squash in the elevator because none of them wanted to be next to the Professor and his whip. He got out at the Sea Lion Deck, but Nim, Selkie and Fred went up to the Flamingo Deck above, where the café chairs were set up around the top of the waterslide, like a theatre balcony for the show at the pool below.

There was a person in every chair, and when Nim looked down she saw people sitting all around the Waterslide Pool and standing behind all the way out to the railings. There were more people than Nim had thought could fit on the ship. For a minute she wanted to turn and run. Fred forgot his sulks and raced up her leg to her shoulder.

Then the three friends walked through the café to the top of the waterslide.

Fred rubbed his spiny head under her chin. Nim put her hand on Selkie's shoulder. They were ready. They looked down to see the Professor on a stage beside the pool.

'Ladies and Gentlemen!' he shouted. 'Instead of my

usual lecture this morning, I'll be demonstrating how well I've trained a seal and a lizard – by allowing a mere child to do the show!'

Dozens of kids waved and screamed, 'Me! Pick me!'

The Professor ignored them and sat down in a chair near the box, his whip across his knees. 'This had better be good!' he snarled.

~

FRED WHIZZED DOWN the waterslide into the pool. Nim followed – and then Selkie whooshed down the curves and *whumphed* in with a tidal-wave splash. The audience squealed, clapped and cheered. The people in the front three rows were soaked.

Nim climbed out of the pool to the front stage. She took a deep breath and wondered if her voice would come out at all.

Then she saw Erin and Ben in the very front row – and beside and behind them, all the kids from the Kids' Klub. Suddenly she knew she could do it.

'Ladies and Gentlemen!' she shouted. 'Allow me to present my sea lion friend, Selkie!'

Selkie pulled herself
up on the side of the pool
and bowed her head to the left,
to the right, and straight ahead.
Everyone in the audience felt as if she'd
bowed to them.

'And,' Nim continued, 'the handsomest, funniest,
smartest marine iguana in the whole world: Fred!'

Fred had to scramble up the steps and onto Nim's
shoulder before he could nod at the audience, but when he

did, Erin and Ben cheered so loudly that everyone else had to join in.

'Statue!' Nim shouted, and Selkie sat up as tall and still as the sea lions on the chessboard.

Nim threw four fish and Selkie expertly caught every one. Fred caught lettuce and chunks of fruit.

'Yay, Fred!' the kids all cheered.

Selkie kissed Erin, and Fred sneezed on Ben.

'Yuck, Fred!' the kids all called, laughing as they clapped.

Selkie, Nim and Fred dived into the pool and played coconut soccer with a ball instead of a coconut.

'Hooray!' shouted the audience.

The ship was going slowly down a strait between mainland and islands. High in the distance was a dark speck that just might be a frigate bird.

'Throw the ball here!' the kids all shouted, until the Professor got out of his seat to glare at them.

Nim hopped out of the pool and threw a rubber ring back in. Fred nosed it up from the bottom and Selkie tossed it back.

'Throw something into the pool!' Nim called. 'And they'll play catch!' A boy threw in his watch. 'It's waterproof!' he shouted, and the crowd cheered as Selkie tossed it back.

Nim looked at Erin. Erin nodded and threw in a banana.

Fred grabbed it, Selkie threw it – and Fred gulped it.

'Hooray for Fred!' Kelvin cheered. He still didn't want to touch Fred, but he was glad he'd rescued him.

Out of the corner of her eye, Nim saw Ben slip away from the crowd and down the stairs, pulling on the Troppo Tourist jacket as he ran.

She also saw that the black speck in the sky had grown into a frigate bird outline.

There was only one fish left in the bucket.

But then Erin pulled out the basket of papier mâché fish she and Nim had made. She threw the first one to Nim, twirling it high in the air. Nim caught it and threw it the same way to Selkie, who tossed it to Fred, who tossed it back to Nim as Erin threw the next one to Selkie.

The Professor stood up to take a picture, his whip tucked under his arm.

Nim threw the fish to him.

The crowd gasped as an enormous black bird, wings as wide across as the Professor was tall, swooped in to snatch the papier mâché fish. The Professor gasped and ducked as the bird's left wing brushed his face and its head went through the loop of the dangling whip.

'Introducing Galileo!' Nim shouted, throwing him the last real fish for a reward.

Galileo dropped the papier mâché fish onto the Professor's head, caught the real one, and soared upwards with the whip bouncing on his bright red chest – till it slipped away and sank into the cold waters of New York Harbour.

The Professor bellowed with rage. He was so angry he forgot to even pretend that he was in charge of the show.

'If you planned this…' he screamed at Nim.

Selkie leapt up and smashed down so hard in front of him that the front rows got soaked all over again. The Professor was drenched, standing in a puddle of water.

'I'm warning you!' he shrieked.

'Play nicely, Selkie!' said Nim, and threw her the ball again.

Selkie leapt up as she hit the ball back, straight and hard at the Professor. He threw his arms up to catch it, skidded in the puddle of water and fell down hard on his bottom.

Fred scurried to Selkie's head, and sneezed in the Professor's face.

The audience laughed and cheered as if it were a clown act.

'Naughty Selkie!' Nim said lovingly. 'Naughty Fred!'

'Yuck, Fred!' the kids shouted gleefully.

Selkie whuffled, and put her flippers up to her face as if she were crying.

The audience cheered louder than ever.

The Professor's eyes went narrow and his face was purple red. 'That's the end of the show!' he shouted.

Now the ship was going under a bridge. The land was close enough that they could see the cubes and rectangles of buildings, but there was still a bit further to go.

'Encore!' shouted Erin, and the whole audience took it up, 'Encore, encore! More, more, more!'

Nim blew her shell whistle. Selkie pulled herself out of the pool. Fred scrambled up beside her.

'I said the show is over!' the Professor screamed.

'Encore, encore!' the audience screamed back.

Selkie and Fred climbed onto the stage.

Nim blew her whistle again. Selkie dived in, rolling and porpoising around the pool, as if she were loosening up for the swim of her life. Nim dived in and Selkie dived under her so that Nim was riding on her back.

Nim blew the whistle again and Fred dived too, right onto Selkie's back and up to Nim's shoulder.

The audience cheered, the Professor glowered, and Nim, Selkie and Fred climbed out of the pool.

The ship slowed down still more.

The Professor moved towards Nim. His eyes were as narrow and glinting as a knife. 'These animals are going back to their cages,' he snarled. 'Get into the elevator.'

Nim, Selkie and Fred walked towards it, very, very slowly.

'Wait!' Erin screamed. 'I want to pat Selkie goodbye!'

'And Fred!'

'We want to pat Selkie!'

'Me too, me too!'

Fred scrambled back to Nim's shoulder as the kids swarmed around them, patting Selkie and hugging Nim. Some of the adults joined in, and a few who couldn't get close enough handed Erin money to give to Nim. 'A show like that deserves a tip!' said one soaking-wet woman.

Erin shoved the money into Nim's extra-safe pocket, then whispered something to the little pig-tailed girl from the Kids' Klub. The girl ran to the Professor and tagged him on the back. 'Spider!' she shouted.

Then Erin and Nim jumped into the elevator.

As the doors shut Nim saw the mob of kids squeal and surge towards the left-hand rail, with the Professor spluttering and bellowing in the middle of them, locked in as firmly as if in a cage.

Nim pushed the button for the Dolphin Deck, the lowest level with an outside deck. The elevator stopped.

'Ready?' asked Erin.

Nim couldn't speak. She nodded.

Erin burst out of the doors and raced to the left-hand side of the ship. 'The Statue of Liberty!' she screamed. 'Look at all the birds around the Statue of Liberty!'

There weren't many passengers down on this deck and

most had been staring out over the left hand side at the great green statue. But now everyone turned to watch a flock of brightly coloured birds – parrots, rainbow doves, flamingos, eagles and a toucan, all led by an enormous black frigate bird – soar into the grey sky and wheel around the statue's uplifted torch.

No one looked across. If they had, they might have seen a sea lion and a girl with an iguana on her shoulder slip out of the elevator to the right-hand side of the ship.

Every one of them missed the most spectacular trick of all, the one where Selkie flopped onto a deck chair against the railing and pulled herself into her best ever flipper-stand. They missed seeing Fred climb to her flippers and be launched from his own personal diving board as Selkie dived over the ship's rail and down, down, down into the water of New York Harbour.

And they missed seeing Nim take the biggest breath of her life and jump.

Chapter 17

THE WATER WAS as cold as ice-cream. Nim gasped as she sank deep and swirling in the waves of the ship's huge wake, but then Selkie was below her, strong and solid, nudging her up through the murky grey.

Nim spluttered out cold water and breathed in warm air. Fred scrambled onto her shoulder; she settled herself on Selkie's back and wrapped her arms around the sea lion's neck. The ship was already far ahead of them. Selkie could swim faster than most boats could sail, but she had to move slowly with Nim on her back. They still had a long way to go.

To Nim's left was the statue of the enormous green woman with the confused tropical birds circling her torch. Beside her was another small island with square red-brick buildings. Straight ahead was the huge city-island they were trying to reach: an island covered with shining grey towers as tall as the ship was long. It was as different from Nim's island as any place in the world could be.

'YOU,' ALEX SAID to herself when she woke up, 'are the most mixed-up, muddle-headed, woolly-witted woman in the world.'

Alex agreed.

'You were living in a paradise with people you love, and you ran away.'

'It's the worst thing I've ever done,' Alex agreed.

'So what are you going to do about it?'

'Go back,' said Alex. 'Go straight back, say I'm sorry, and make things right again.'

'You'll go straight to the airport when you get off the ship?'

Alex thought for a second. 'First I'll go to see Delia.'

~

HALFWAY AROUND THE world, Jack was fast asleep, stretched out behind a row of chairs on the Isla Grande airport floor. It wasn't much more comfortable than the raft, but Jack didn't want to leave the airport and miss the plane. He didn't want anything to keep him from finding Nim and Alex.

~

NIM HADN'T THOUGHT there'd be so many boats. There were three ships ahead of the Troppo Tourists, boxy orange ferries, small bright yellow water taxis, sleek yachts, and more than a dozen sailboats. Small planes darted overhead, and a helicopter whirred so fiercely that Selkie forgot about Nim and dived down deep. Nim and Fred floated off in surprise. Suddenly the waves seemed higher and the current seemed stronger – and Nim was colder and more tired than she'd ever been before.

'Selkie!' she shouted. 'Come back!'

Selkie glided up from below, whuffling apologetically as Nim and Fred slid back on.

The buildings got closer. The closer they got, the bigger they grew. They looked as tall as Fire Mountain, and they covered the island so thickly Nim wondered how people could walk in between them.

A motorboat roared by; Selkie swerved out of its way, but two sailboats were following, with a whole fleet of other sailboats chasing them, and a yellow water taxi zipping through the middle.

'We've got to get out of here!' Nim said.

Selkie veered to the right, away from the racing sailboats. A little grey-and-white tugboat, with red trim and a fat and friendly shape, was coming that way. No matter which way Selkie veered, the tug kept chugging straight towards them. Its engines were slowing, and there was a man standing at the bow waving while two others rushed to unclip the life rings.

'Hang on!' the captain shouted from a loudspeaker in the wheelhouse. 'We're coming!'

Nim and Selkie had been friends since Nim was a baby. They both knew what the other was feeling, and now they both knew that they might never get to shore without help.

'And if they try to put us in jail, we'll just have to escape again!' Nim told Selkie and Fred, trying to sound braver than she felt.

The tug was nearly there. The men tossed out the life rings; the youngest man threw off his jacket and shoes and jumped in. Nim slipped off Selkie, Fred slipped off Nim and they all swam towards the boat.

'Over here!' shouted one of the men, running to the tug's low, flat back section. 'Daniel, bring her around to the stern!'

'Right!' the young man shouted, as he swam desperately towards Nim. 'Don't worry! I'm coming!'

With Daniel on one side and Selkie on the other, Nim swam to the tug.

The two men on deck threw themselves down, reaching over the side to Nim. She grabbed their arms and they

 pulled her up on board. Daniel followed. Nim was coughing, spluttering and shaking, and her teeth were chattering so hard she could barely speak. 'Please get Fred!'

Daniel rushed to the edge. 'There's someone else out there?'

Nim pointed. Fred was riding on top of one of the life rings.

'That's Fred?' Daniel asked. He was shivering a bit too. 'I guess he can't hang onto the life ring if we pull it in?'

Nim shook her head.

'Well,' said Daniel, as he got ready to jump in again, 'I sure hope Fred appreciates this.'

But at that moment, Selkie came up under Fred, and soccer-tossed him onto the deck. Then, with a mighty leap, she flopped up beside him.

The older man came back from the wheelhouse with a blanket, and wrapped it snugly around Nim. 'I take it they're friends of yours?' he asked, as Fred scurried to Nim's shoulder and Selkie settled herself protectively behind them.

Nim nodded.

'Okay. Because otherwise that's one lost sea lion, let alone the iguana. So what happened?'

'I fell off a boat,' Nim said, pointing vaguely towards the disappearing sailboats.

'You fell off a boat and nobody noticed?'

Nim nodded, her teeth still chattering.

'Hmm. That's not the whole story, is it?'

'No,' Nim said honestly.

'Well, let's get you warmed up and we'll work out what to do with you. What about some hot chocolate? And Daniel, you're the skinniest – how about finding her one of your spare T-shirts so we can dry her clothes?'

Nim went into the cabin and changed into Daniel's T-shirt. It came down to her knees like a dress, so she could hang her own clothes out over the line to dry in the sun.

'Now,' said the older man, when Nim reappeared. 'Let's start with names. You can call me Ivan, and you are?'

'Nim Rusoe.'

'And where are your parents, Miss Nim Rusoe? Who am I going to call to say we've fished you out of the harbour and could they please come and pick you up?'

'My mum's dead,' said Nim, 'and you can't call my dad. But I'm looking for my friend Alex Rover.'

'Alex Rover, like the author?' asked Ivan.

'Nim, like *Nim's Island*?' asked Daniel, pointing to a water taxi zipping towards the shore. On its side was an enormous poster of a girl with a spyglass at her eye and an iguana on her shoulder, leaning out from the top of a palm tree while a sea lion splashed in the cove below. *Nim's Island* was written around the top, and 'the newest by ALEX ROVER' in even bigger letters underneath.

Nim's brain couldn't believe what her eyes were seeing. It was like looking into her rainwater pool and seeing a strange, almost-Nim, reflection looking back at her.

'Yes,' she whispered. 'That's me.'

Chapter 18

JACK CHECKED HIS email at the airport again before his flight left. There was still nothing from Alex or Nim. Before, Jack hadn't known if he was more scared or angry. Now he knew: he was just plain scared. Because it didn't make sense. Alex would never have taken Nim without telling him. And Nim would never have meant to leave without telling him.

But what else could have happened? What if they'd been kidnapped by the supply plane pilot? What if he'd come right across the world to find them and they were still somewhere near the island?

Maybe he should jump straight onto a plane home the instant he landed.

'I've got this far,' he decided. 'I'll look for them in the city first.'

But as the plane roared up the runway, Jack suddenly remembered that if someone's name wasn't in his email address book, the message went into the Trash unless it had the words "science" or "research" in the subject line. And the Trash folder had blinked every time he'd checked his emails.

Alex and Nim didn't know that.

There could be an email from them in the Trash right now! Jack thought bitterly.

But he'd have to wait till the plane landed before he could check.

~

IVAN WAS JUST about to phone Delia Defoe to tell her about Nim, when a call came in over their radio. A big cruise ship needed a tugboat to tow it up the Hudson River to its dock.

'I guess we could take you with us,' said Ivan. 'Maybe someone could meet you at the cruise ship terminal.'

'No!' Nim exclaimed. 'I can't go anywhere near the cruise ships!'

Ivan looked at her shrewdly. 'You might have to tell us a bit more of your story, young Nim.'

'There's a Professor on the ship. He kidnapped Selkie, and he wanted Fred too. He said that was the law because of the Foundation for Intelligent, Unique and Interesting Animals – but Selkie's been my friend since I was three, and Fred since he was hatched…they can't belong to this Foundation, and go to live with people to study them. They just can't.'

'So you jumped overboard to save them?' asked Ivan.

Nim nodded.

Daniel whistled.

'Well,' said Ivan, 'you've got the courage of your convictions, that's for sure. I don't see that we've got any choice but to get you where you're going – sea lion, iguana and all. And until the police have sorted out this Professor and his Foundation we'll help you steer clear of him.'

'We could drop you off somewhere else,' Daniel suggested, 'if someone could meet you.'

Ivan phoned Papyrus Publishing. When he asked to speak to Delia Defoe he was put through to her voicemail, and when he phoned back and tried to explain that he had Nim with him and that she needed to find Alex Rover, he was put through to a special recorded announcement about publicity for Alex Rover's new book. When he tried a third time and explained how urgent it was, he was told that Papyrus Publishing never ever gave out an author's address or phone number.

'I'm afraid you'll simply have to go to the publishing house,' said Ivan. 'We could put you in a cab.'

'I don't think a cab would take Selkie,' Daniel said.

'Selkie can't stay behind!' Nim protested, and Selkie barked 'NO!'

'I'll phone my sister-in-law Carla,' said Daniel. 'You'd all fit in her delivery van.'

He picked up his phone. Nim could faintly hear Carla on the other end, 'A sea lion? Are you for real?'

The radio crackled. 'The cruise ship's waiting. Is there a problem?'

Daniel grinned as he put away his phone. 'We're in luck – Carla's down near the water taxi dock right now.'

'Give me five minutes!' Ivan said into the radio. 'We've got an emergency delivery to the water taxi dock.'

'Does Carla like sea lions?' Nim asked anxiously.

'Sure! She's just never met one.'

'And marine iguanas?'

'Who wouldn't love Fred?'

Fred smirked, and went on munching the salad Ivan had made him.

Nim's clothes were nearly dry. She took them off the line and changed in the cabin as they pulled into the dock.

Ivan handed her a card when she came back to the wheelhouse. 'You'll be fine with Carla. But this has got my name and phone number – you call me if you've got any problems. Call us if you don't have any problems! We want to hear you got there safe.'

'Thank you,' said Nim. 'And thank you for the sandwich and hot chocolate.' If she ever did get back to the island, she thought, maybe she could take some hot chocolate with her.

'Here's my number too,' said Daniel.

'And thank you for rescuing me,' Nim said.

'Anyone jumps off a ship into New York Harbour to rescue their friends,' said Daniel, 'I'd be proud to rescue them.'

'Just don't make a habit of it!' Ivan warned, giving her a warm hug. 'And don't forget to call us.'

The tug bumped up against the dock. Daniel jumped down, and Selkie, Nim and Fred followed.

~

THEY GOT OFF at a park, with a wide stretch of green grass that ended at a path as smooth and hard as rock, and so crowded that everyone had to move with determination and speed. Nim had never imagined that so many people could fit into the same place at the same time.

While they walked they talked on phones, to each other, to themselves; some used words Nim couldn't understand

and languages she'd never heard. They drank cans of soft drink and cups of coffee, ate ice-cream on sticks and hot dogs and pretzels, carried purses and briefcases and fat bags with shopping or small dogs inside – and somehow they hardly ever bumped into each other.

'Come on,' said Daniel. 'Carla's waiting. It'll be fine.'

Nim took a deep breath. Fred curled himself tighter around her neck. Selkie pressed hard against her. They followed Daniel down the path.

Next to the path was a road, and on the road there were cars. Lots of yellow cars, and lots of every-other-colour-in-the-world cars. Some were going one way and some were going the other, but just when Nim thought they'd meet *smash* in the middle, they slipped safely on by.

Nim had seen pictures of cars, but she'd never heard the noise or smelled the smell. The smell was hot and the noise was hotter, and just when she thought it couldn't get any louder there was a high-pitched siren, a roaring noise like a sea lion bull, and a huge red truck screamed past.

Selkie didn't like this place with all its strange noises, and she wanted to get through it as fast as she could. She galumphed off the path onto the road.

Cars honked and brakes screeched.

'Selkie!' shouted Nim, dashing into the road after her.

'Wait!' shouted Daniel, grabbing Nim's arm.

'What part of *DON'T WALK!* don't you understand?' shouted a taxi driver at the people dashing across while the cars stopped for Selkie.

Sellkie barked crossly and flopped back up onto the path.

'It's Nim and the sea lion!' shouted a woman on the opposite side of the street.

'Is that who you're supposed to be?' a man called. 'Are you supposed to be Nim?'

'Great publicity stunt!' cheered another man.

Then the cars stopped, and so did the flashing sign of a little red man walking. As everyone stepped onto the road the sign below lit up to show a little white man walking.

So that's how they know when to do it! thought Nim, as she stepped up onto the sidewalk on the other side.

They hurried on through a little park, ignoring the flowers and cool splashing fountain. At the end of the park was an enormous bull.

Selkie barked and wouldn't go on.

'It's okay!' Nim coaxed. 'He's just a statue!'

Selkie froze into her statue trick, and the people who were lined up to have their pictures taken with the bull ran over to take pictures of Selkie, too.

'Is that a real sea lion?'

'Is it safe?'

'Of course,' said Nim, and a woman rushed up to stand beside her while her friend took a picture. Fred reached over and gulped the top off her ice-cream cone.

'Sorry,' said Nim, though Fred wasn't sorry at all.

There was a whisper of excitement, and more people kept coming and taking more pictures.

'Got to keep moving, guys!' Daniel said.

'Where are you going?' a long-haired man called.

'Papyrus Publishing.'

'Have you got the address?' asked a grandmotherly woman, writing it on the back of her shopping list. 'My son works there.'

'That's a long way uptown,' said a woman in a red suit. 'How're you going to get them there?'

'You could take the subway!' suggested the long-haired man.

'You can't take a sea lion on the subway!' said the red-suited woman. 'You need to call one of those cabs that takes dogs.'

'My sister uses those to take her dogs to day care,' said a carpenter walking past. 'I'll call her and get their number.'

'Thanks,' said Daniel, 'but we've already got a ride.' They crossed the road to a woman opening the back door of a van covered with pictures of dogs and the sign *Carla's Canine Cakes*.

Chapter 19

CARLA KISSED DANIEL, hugged Nim, patted Selkie and almost patted Fred, all at once and all while she was talking. 'Glad to help out. I thought Daniel must be kidding, but you're for real all right. You can tell me your story on the way – where is it you need to go?'

Daniel gave her the address, ruffled Nim's hair, and jogged back to the dock where the tugboat was waiting.

'We've got a few deliveries to do on the way,' said Carla. 'Cakes can't wait! I've stacked up the boxes so the sea lion can fit – Selkie, is it? – Selkie, can you hop right in there, honey? Just don't squish the boxes!'

Selkie flopped in to the back of the van, in front of the stacked cake boxes. It was cool, and if she sat up high she'd be able to see out the back window. She gave a honk of approval.

'And what about this little guy?' Carla asked, pointing to Fred.

'He's not going to climb all over
the boxes, is he?'

'He might,' said Nim.

'Okay, Freddy, in the front with
Fritz. And you too, Nim. Fritz, stop
barking, I'm sure Fred's much nicer
than he looks. Buckle up and off we
go; we've got a bunch of cakes to get
where they're going.'

Fritz was a dachshund, a short-legged long-bodied dog
about the same size and shape as Fred. At first he squeezed
himself against Carla, but then he wiggled up against Nim.
Fred sneezed jealously; Fritz barked in surprise and then
crawled across Nim to the side window so he could stand
and look out, carefully ignoring Fred.

Fred did the same, carefully ignoring Fritz.

A bus went by. It was completely covered by the same
Nim's Island picture as the water taxi.

Carla laughed. 'Would you look at that! How do you
feel about people staring at you all over Manhattan?'

'A bit strange,' said Nim, because it seemed more polite
than saying it made her feel sick.

'So?' asked Carla. 'Spill the story. What's a kid doing
in New York City all on her lonesome? Or another way
to put it, what's a kid doing with a sea lion and an iguana
and their picture on a bus? You know, I see a lot of strange
things driving around this town, but I've never seen
that before. Now, where did I put the address for that

Dalmatian cake? There it is, under your feet, just grab it for me, will you?'

A yellow car with a *Nim's Island* sign on the back blared its horn.

'Hey!' Carla shouted back. 'I've got the real thing in here, so just watch who you're honking.'

Fritz barked in agreement. Fred sneezed.

'Here we are!' Carla exclaimed a few minutes later, turning into a side street and stopping with a jolt. 'We'll have to get Selkie out so I can reach the cake...will you guys be okay while I run it up? It's only half a block, twelfth floor, this says – won't take me more than ten minutes.'

'We'll be fine,' said Nim.

But Selkie had seen a pond.

It was a wide shallow pond in a small park, with a splashing fountain in the middle. Two boys and a girl were standing in the fountain, and a mother and baby were slapping at the shallow water at the pond's edge. Selkie galumphed down the sidewalk, through a big marble arch, and cannonballed in. The pond was even more shallow than she'd realised, and instead of sinking down she skidded right across to the other side.

The baby laughed and clapped his hands. His mother whisked him up and stood ready to run.

'She won't hurt him!' Nim called, jogging across with Fred and Fritz close behind.

'Okay,' said the mum, and after a while she put the baby down again to splash and watch.

Selkie rolled on her back and Nim splashed water over her dusty belly. Fred waded across to the fountain. Fritz followed him, until Fred climbed into the jet of spray and was bubbled up and over the edge.

'Cool!' said one of the boys.

'Is he yours?' asked the other.

'And the sea lion?' asked the girl.

'They're my friends,' said Nim.

'Do you belong to a circus?'

'We don't belong to anyone,' said Nim. 'We're just us.'

But now she could see Carla crossing the street back towards the park. 'Fred!' she called, 'Selkie! Fritz! Time to get going!'

The kids ran back to the van with them, waving goodbye as they drove off.

ALEX SAW THE Statue of Liberty out her cabin window as the ship sailed past. She had nothing to pack but the pyjamas and toothbrush she'd bought, and the book that Delia had sent her.

For the first time, she opened her new book and began to read.

The ship slowed to nearly a full stop. The engines were barely purring. There seemed to be quite a long wait before a tugboat towed it to the dock.

Alex began to smile as she read.

The ship docked. Ropes were run out and looped over the bollards on the dock; the gangplank slammed down.

Alex looked up, wishing she were reading the book aloud to Jack and Nim, with Fred, Selkie and Chica looking on.

People were walking past her window, wheeling suitcases and carrying backpacks.

The mother of the next-door children called, 'But I asked you to pack this morning!' and the children shouted, 'We were busy!'

Alex went on reading.

Virginia knocked on the door to tell her it was time to leave the ship and ask if she needed help with her bags.

'No thanks,' said Alex, and went to stand in the queue to say goodbye to the crew. It was a long line, and she went on reading as she stood.

She shook hands with the captain, and saw that the family in the cabins next door had lined up behind her. The children looked as bouncy and friendly as they'd sounded through the walls, and Alex wished she'd been brave enough to meet them. She joined an even longer line to show her passport and leave the dock – and very nearly finished the book.

'But I do know the ending,' she reminded herself. 'At least, I think I do.'

Suddenly she could hardly wait to get off the ship and sort out the ending to her even newer story.

~

'DO YOU SEE that woman's book?' Ben asked Erin.

Erin stared hard. She read the title and she felt a bit sick. 'Do you think Nim just read it and made everything up?'

'She couldn't have. She had Fred.'

'And Selkie.'

'It's still very weird.'

'What's even weirder is that woman's wearing pants like Nim's. *Nobody* has pants like Nim's.'

'And she hasn't got a suitcase.'

'As if she got on in a hurry…'

'…like Nim.'

'Do you think it could be?'

'Let's ask her!'

But by the time all their passports were stamped and bags checked, Alex had vanished.

Ben and Erin followed their parents and the twins out to stand in line for a taxi. The first one to pull in had a sign on the roof: *Nim's Island by ALEX ROVER. In stores July 7!*

'That's today,' said Erin.

'So the only person on the ship who could already be reading it…'

'…is Alex Rover.'

Ben started to giggle. 'Can you imagine what she'll say when she sees Nim!'

'And Selkie and Fred!'

~

JACK'S PLANE DIDN'T go all the way to New York; he had to change planes twice. He rushed to check his email again at an airport computer as he waited for the last plane. This time he went straight to the Trash bin. It was crammed with messages.

As he skimmed down the list, his heart started thumping so fast he could hardly breathe.

From: erin@kidmail.com
To: jack.rusoe@explorer.net
Date: Wednesday July 7, 11:30am
Subject: Very very urgent about Nim

Dear Mr. Rusoe

I'm the girl who sent Nim's emails to you before.
I hope you don't think I'm rude but I think it's very
mean that you haven't written to Nim yet. Anyway,
I thought you'd like to know that the ship is in New
York now and it's going to dock in about half an hour.
We're getting off at the cruise ship terminal but Nim
and Selkie and Fred jumped off when everyone was
looking at the Statue of Liberty.

'Jumped off the ship?' Jack exclaimed.

Nim didn't ask me to write to you this time but
I hope it's okay because she's worried that you're
angry at her about Alex. And she's my friend so I
don't want her to be upset, so could you please write
to her soon. I guess she can check her email when
she finds Alex.

From Erin Caritas

Jack felt hot and cold and didn't know if he was going
to be sick or explode, or maybe both at the same time. He
read the email again even though every word was already
burned into his brain, especially 'jumped off the ship', and
'when she finds Alex'.

Then he went down through all the emails that had gone straight into the Trash every time he'd checked for mail from Nim or Alex.

He found all five messages that Nim had asked Erin to write. When he'd finished reading he knew that:

- Nim, Selkie and Fred had jumped off a ship in the middle of New York Harbour about two hours ago
- They weren't with Alex

There were lots more things that he didn't know, but the most important were:

- Did Nim, Selkie and Fred drown when they jumped off the ship?
- If they hadn't drowned, where were they now?
- Where was Alex?

The other things he really wanted to know but would worry about later were:

- Why did they get onto the ship?
- How did they get onto the ship?
- When did they get onto the ship?
- Why did Alex leave?

But the most important question of all he couldn't even ask because no one knew the answer:

- Would they all find each other again?

To: erin@kidmail.com
From: jack.rusoe@explorer.net
Date: Wednesday July 7, 12:01pm
Subject: Re: Very very urgent about Nim

Dear Erin

Do you really mean that Nim jumped off a ship and swam to land?

I'm arriving in New York at 6:00 this evening on Flight 123. If you talk to Nim please tell her.

I'm very sorry I didn't read your emails before.

Yours truly,

Jack Rusoe

P.S. Thank you for being Nim's friend.

He started another email.

From: jack.rusoe@explorer.net
To: aka@incognito.net

The airport loudspeaker crackled. 'Passenger Jack Rusoe, please go to Boarding Gate 46 immediately. Your flight is about to leave.'

Jack left the computer and raced to the gate. 'Five more hours till I'm there,' he thought.

It was going to be the longest five hours of his life.

# *Chapter 20*

CARLA DROVE NIM and her friends past old buildings, new buildings, buildings of carved stone, buildings of shiny glass, and building after building whose tops were high above the clouds. None of them were where Alex's books were published.

How would I ever have found Delia Defoe by myself? Nim wondered. And if I couldn't find her, how would I ever find Alex?

They passed banks, dress shops, camera shops, jewellery shops, postcard shops, toy shops, pet shops, hotels, cafés, and stands on the street corners selling handbags or sunglasses or snacks and drinks. They saw flags waving, neon signs flashing, steps going down into the ground and steam hissing up from a hole in the path, the way it did from the Hissing Stones when Fire Mountain was getting angry.

They stopped at traffic lights and watched the people crossing.

'Isn't it funny,' Nim said, 'There are so many people – and none of them are ever the same!'

'That's what makes life interesting, honey,' said Carla.

'But what I want to see is the apartment waiting for this poodle birthday cake…don't yap, Fritz, poodles are nice, too. Let's see, if I turn here, go down this street, and now… oh dear, that was exactly what I didn't want to do. Okay, we'll have to park here and walk. You guys can hop out and stretch if you want, better put Fritz on his leash – does Fred have a leash?'

'He can go on my shoulder,' said Nim.

'Okay, don't go far, I'll be as quick as I can.' Carla opened the back of the van to let Selkie out, grabbed the cake box and raced off. Nim and the others followed more slowly, with Selkie pressed close to Nim's side.

On the corner a man was selling pretzels. The pretzels were like bread twisted into knots and covered with salt. Fred liked salt. He leaned out from Nim's shoulder and chomped half a pretzel from the stand.

'That'll be one dollar!' said the man.

I don't have any money! Nim thought, but then she remembered the tips Erin had dropped into her pocket as they got into the elevator. She showed them to the pretzel seller.

'Too much!' he said, taking one green piece and giving her back the rest. Nim bought a bottle of water too, and she still had money left.

They crossed the road, turned the corner – and walked into a solid wall of people. Most of them tried to jump out of Selkie's way, though they were too jammed in to jump far.

The people were staring at giant screens on the fronts

of buildings on both sides of the street. Some of the screens had pictures that changed from one thing to another and back again; others had brightly lit words running across them, starting over again as soon as they'd finished.

One of the running signs said: ALEX ROVER'S *NIM'S ISLAND* RELEASED TODAY.

Nim felt as if the only things that were real were the feel of Fred's spine under her chin and the warmth of Selkie's shoulder.

'Let's get back to the van,' she said, but they were squashed in so tight there was barely room to turn around.

'Whoof!' Selkie barked, 'Whoof-WHOOF!'

The crowd shifted just enough for Nim to get through – but then more people noticed Selkie and Fred, and crowded closer to see.

'They're from Alex Rover's new book!'

'No, they must be filming a movie!'

More people crushed closer. A policeman whistled. Selkie stopped, but the whistle wasn't for her. It was to make the cars stop so Selkie and Nim could cross, with their long parade following behind.

'Where are we going?' a girl asked.

'Back to Carla's van," said Nim. 'And then to find Alex Rover.'

'We're on TV!' shrieked a boy, leaping in front of Nim to wave to a man walking backwards with a camera on his shoulder.

Some people stopped following her then, but others

came closer to ask about Alex. One man pushed his way through with a pen and a book, and asked Nim to sign it. It was Alex's book – and even though looking at it made Nim feel sorry, ashamed and confused, when she read Alex's name, she felt a tiny trickle of hope that maybe Alex would still like her after all.

The man kept on asking till Nim scribbled her name across the face of the girl who was supposed to be her.

'Can I have your autograph too?' a boy asked, but just as other people started pulling out pieces of paper, notebooks and hats, Fred sneezed. Hard.

Everyone stepped back.

Fred looked smug as they met Carla and started off again. The van crawled through the traffic. 'We're nearly there,' Carla explained. 'What we're going to do is loop around, drop off this dog-that-looks-like-a-cat cake – Stop yapping, Fritz, though you're right, who'd want a dog that looks like a cat? But this customer does, so that's what they're getting, and then we'll get Nim where she needs to be.'

Carla turned where the road met a wide green park. Nim saw soft grass, flowers, tall trees and hills. It was like the fresh green heart of this hot busy city.

In the park, people walked and dreamed, lay on the grass, jogged, roller bladed, rode bikes and horses. There were mothers with babies, fathers with toddlers, grandparents with grandchildren, mothers and fathers with little kids and big kids and almost grown-up kids.

Families! thought Nim, and suddenly she didn't want to see any more.

~

CARLA PARKED IN a row of horses and carriages in front of a palace. It looked like a picture in a book Nim had at home. 'Don't go away!' Carla said, letting them all out again to get the dog-that-looked-like-a-cat cake. 'I'll just be a minute!'

Selkie honked in surprise at the horses. She'd never seen animals with such long legs. A big grey horse whinnied back, and Selkie lolloped over to meet it.

'You're a long way from home!' the driver said to Selkie. 'It's a good thing Mabel likes tourists.' He rubbed the horse's neck affectionately.

Mabel and Selkie sniffed noses. Fred and Fritz gulped some popcorn they'd found on the ground.

Nim was the only one who couldn't enjoy the horses and carriages, the golden fountain or the palace, the brilliant sunshine or the green park. Because soon she'd be at Alex's publisher, and if Delia Defoe couldn't help her, she had no idea at all what she was going to do next.

Carla bustled back, looking flushed and cross. 'Turns out they wanted two cakes! Would have been nice if they'd told me when they ordered! So I'm thinking…do you want to go back to the shop with me, and then I can go in to find this Delia with you?'

But Nim couldn't wait any longer. 'We can go in by ourselves,' she said, though she was suddenly more afraid than she'd been ever since she stood at the railing to dive off the ship.

'Okay then…but don't think I'm dumping you off for good. I'll just be about an hour – plenty of time to sort out if this Delia gal can help you. Then I'll come back and see what's happening, and you can all come and stay with me till you find your friend or your dad or whoever.'

'We can stay with you?" Nim asked, amazed.

'Well, I'm hardly going to let you sleep out in Central Park! For one thing Daniel would never speak to me again. Though I warn you, at my house it'll be a squish.'

Nim tried to say thank you, but her throat was even more choked now than when she'd been afraid.

'Here we are!' Carla pulled up in front of a tall, shining building with Alex Rover's name hung in a banner across a window display of *Nim's Island* books. She gave Nim a card, hugged her hard and patted Fred before opening the back door for Selkie. 'Here's my number in case you need it. Remember I'll be back in an hour.'

She pulled back into the traffic, sticking her head out the window to shout once more, 'Don't worry!'

'I won't,' Nim lied, as she waved goodbye.

She pushed the door.

It was a heavy glass door, and when Nim stepped in, another door followed close behind, so there was only just enough space for Nim and Fred. Selkie threw herself at the second door so hard that all the doors spun around, and Nim ended up back on the street where she'd begun.

She tried again. This time she got into the building, and so did Selkie.

Books in glass cases were on every side, up to the ceiling. Nim knew she was in the right place.

Three men were sitting behind a desk.

'Oh my goodness!' said the first.

'You'd think publicity could have told us!' said the second.

'Let me guess,' said the third. 'You must be Nim!'

'Yes,' said Nim, 'I need to see Alex Rover.'

The men looked at each other.

'Get Delia Defoe,' said one, and the second man picked up the phone.

'Wait there, sweetie,' said the third, and Nim and Selkie sat down in front of the bookcases. Nim read the titles while Fred stretched out under the shelf. Selkie watched the people coming in and going out through the heavy revolving door.

Elevator doors opened, and a woman stepped out.

'I'm Alex Rover's editor,' she said. 'I appreciate your interest in this book, and I'm very intrigued about how you organised these animals so fast, but Alex Rover doesn't give interviews.'

'I don't want an interview,' said Nim. 'I just have to talk to her.'

'Most people think Alex Rover's a man – why do you think she's a woman?'

'Because she's my friend,' said Nim. 'At least, she was.'

'Well, I could give her your message. Why do you need to see her?'

'To say I'm sorry,' Nim muttered, hiding her face against her knees so Delia wouldn't see her cry.

'Do you mean,' Delia said softly, as if she couldn't quite believe what she was asking, 'that you're the real Nim? And this is truly Fred – and Selkie?'

Nim nodded.

Delia squatted down on the floor beside her, and Nim told her the story; everything except exactly what she'd said to Alex, because she thought Delia wouldn't want to help her if she knew just how horrible Nim had been.

At first Delia looked excited, but as the story went on she looked more and more concerned.

'So now can you tell me how to find Alex?' asked Nim.

'I'd love to,' said Delia. 'The problem is – I don't have any idea.'

Chapter 21

WHEN ALEX FINALLY got out of the cruise ship terminal, she could see the top of the Papyrus Publishing building, tall and shining above the others around it. There was a long queue for taxis, and Alex needed to get there fast. She crossed the highway and started to walk.

She wrote her email to Nim and Jack in her head as she walked. It wasn't easy, but she knew what she had to say. The only thing she didn't know was what their answer would be.

She was thinking about them so hard that sometimes she'd see a girl with hair like Nim's, or a man who walked like Jack, and for half a moment she'd think, They're here!

It was so bad that when she looked in the window of her publisher's building, she thought she saw Selkie sitting in front of the bookcases.

'You,' Alex told herself, 'are going absolutely fruitcake nutty!'

'But,' she added, 'in five more minutes you can email them.'

~

271

'FIRST THINGS FIRST,' Delia was saying to Nim. 'Come up to my office to email Alex and your father – Selkie and Fred can stay down here, can't they?'

Selkie barked and pressed hard against Nim, while Fred scrambled up to her shoulder.

'Okay,' said Delia. 'I guess we can take the freight elevator.'

Suddenly Selkie barked louder and skidded across to the revolving door as fast as she could lollop.

'Selkie!' shouted Nim.

And then she saw Alex.

They raced across the floor and met in the middle, hanging on just as tight as they had when Nim had pulled Alex out of her sinking sailboat. Selkie whuffled around them in a loving circle and Fred climbed up to Alex's shoulder.

'But how?' Alex asked. 'And when?'

'On a ship,' said Nim. 'I'm sorry, I'm so sorry.'

'Where's Jack?'

'I think he's very mad at me. I don't know why I said such terrible things.'

'Do you mean you came *alone*?'

'That's what she means,' said Delia. 'Which is one of the many reasons I'm so happy to meet my best-selling author!'

Alex let go of Nim for just long enough to shake Delia's hand. 'Before we do anything else,' she said, 'could we please email Jack?'

Delia led them around to the freight elevator and they all rode up to Delia's office, with Nim and Alex still both talking at once and trying to explain.

'…and then we jumped off,' said Nim. 'Near the green lady.'

'Jumped off what?' asked Alex, feeling sick.

'The ship,' said Nim.

Alex felt even sicker. 'What ship?' she asked, when she could breathe again.

Nim told her, and Alex told Nim her story, and Nim laughed and cried and Alex cried and laughed, when they realised that Nim had been hiding in a lifeboat right outside Alex's cabin for that whole week.

Then Alex checked her email, and the messages came flooding in. She read through Jack's messages from the last right back to the first. The more she read the paler she got, because Jack was so angry and sad she knew he'd never want to see her again.

'But I told him what happened,' Nim said sadly. 'Erin sent an email every day.'

'Maybe he was too sad to understand,' said Alex.

From: aka@incognito.net
To: jack.rusoe@explorer.com
Date: Wednesday July 7, 2:02pm
Subject: I've found Alex!

Dear Jack

You shouldn't be angry at Alex because it's not her fault that I left. But it's **my** fault **she** left.

I wish you could come too.

We are going down to the sea now so Selkie and Fred can swim in salt water, because they've just been in fountains today. I hope your email is working so you get this and I hope you answer.

Love (as much as Selkie loves us)

Nim

'But what if the Professor tries to catch Selkie again?' Nim asked.

'NO ONE is ever going to take Selkie away again!' said Alex. She looked so fierce that Nim believed her.

~

DELIA'S PHONE RANG. 'There's someone waiting for you downstairs,' she said, and for just a minute both Nim and Alex thought, Jack!

They all rode the freight elevator back down to the lobby, and though it wasn't Jack, Nim was still very glad to see Carla. Fred was glad to see Fritz, and Alex and Delia were glad to meet someone who'd helped Nim. There were more thank yous, more exclaiming and explaining, and then Carla and Fritz dashed off to start baking tomorrow's cakes.

A long white car with black windows pulled up in front. The driver got out to open the doors.

'Here's your car,' said Delia. 'Are you sure you don't want me to organise a hotel?'

'Thanks,' said Alex, 'but I'd like to do it myself. It's time I learned to do things like that.'

A boy and a girl with their mother stopped to stare as Alex, Delia, Nim and Fred, and finally Selkie, came out through the revolving doors.

'Look at the sea lion!'

'That kid's got a lizard on her shoulder!'

'Oh, they're just advertising a book,' said the mother.

Nim and Alex looked at each other and laughed so hard they had to lean against the limousine before they could get into it.

Delia waved goodbye as the car pulled out, with Nim and Alex sitting beside each other, Fred on the back of the seat staring out a window, and Selkie sitting on the floor and staring out hers.

Alex pushed a button in the limousine's door and her window rolled down. Nim pushed the button for Selkie, but rolled Fred's down just enough that he could put his head out, and not so far he could fall out by mistake.

'Help yourself to a drink,' the driver said.

There were bottles in a cupboard behind the driver's seat. Nim had to pour the water into a lid for Fred. Selkie could drink hers from the bottle.

The limousine driver politely asked Selkie not to put her head out the window with the bottle in her mouth. Selkie finished her water fast: she liked having her head out of the window.

When they stopped at a light, three dogs crossed the road in front of them.

'WHOOF!' honked Selkie, racing from one window to the next.

'Arf!' the dogs yipped in surprise.

Selkie whuffled happily. Limousines were much nicer than being on her own in the back of a van, trying not to move in case she squashed cakes.

～

THE DRIVER TOOK them to another park a little further up the river from where the tugboat had brought Nim that morning. There was a marina with boats moored all along the wharves: sailboats, motorboats, and some that looked more like floating houses. One had flower boxes at its windows and a 'For Rent' sign on its bow.

'Interesting!' Alex said thoughtfully. 'But I'm starving. Let's get something to eat.'

Fred rubbed his spiky back against her ankle. He'd nearly forgotten how much he liked Alex.

The four of them walked together across the green grass to a café in the middle. They sat at an outside table, where Selkie and Fred could watch the dogs sitting at other tables with their people. Alex ordered fish and chips and salad, but added, 'One fish needs to be raw, please!'

'Of course!' said the waiter, and brought Selkie and Fred a bowl of water to share while they waited.

'I didn't know you had sea lions in New York City,' said the man at the next table.

'We're just visiting,' Alex explained.

'And I love your mother-and-daughter outfits!' his wife exclaimed. 'Did you make them yourself?'

Alex looked embarrassed. 'We're not…'

'Yes,' said Nim.

Alex's eyes filled up with tears. 'We'll have to find somewhere to check emails after dinner,' she said – because even though Nim had forgiven her for leaving, she didn't know if Jack ever could.

'But Selkie and Fred need to swim first,' said Nim, and so when they'd finished, they wandered down to the marina. Fred and Selkie lollopped across the park and into the water – and as they ran, more and more people came to stare.

'Quick!' said Alex, and they raced to the end of a pier where a sign said: 'Kayaks for hire.'

'Have you kayaked before?' the woman asked.

'Of course!' said Alex.

They climbed in and started to paddle. They were splashing as much water as Selkie in a fountain, but somehow they didn't move very far or very fast.

'Are you sure you've done this before?' Nim asked.

'It might have been one of my books,' said Alex. 'I get mixed up.'

Chapter 22

ERIN AND BEN were at the airport with their family, waiting for the plane to take them the rest of the way home. They were early, the plane was late, and they were bored with waiting. Erin wanted to check her email but there were no computers to do it.

'What's so important it can't wait till we get home?' her dad teased.

Erin thought maybe it was time to tell him. 'It's about Nim,' she began.

'She's on TV!' shouted Ben.

'Amazing scenes in New York earlier today,' said the television news above their heads, 'when Times Square played host to a visiting sea lion.'

Erin spun around to see Nim, Selkie and Fred pushing through crowds in the square with the giant computer screens.

'Originally thought to be a publicity stunt for today's release of Alex Rover's new book *Nim's Island*...'

The camera showed a *Nim's Island* bus.

'...events have now taken a dramatic turn, with a

spokesman for the Troppo Tourist Cruise Ship claiming that this girl…' Nim's face filled the screen '…had in fact stowed away and stolen the highly trained, valuable sea lion from their care.'

'Liar!' shouted Ben.

'NIM!' shouted a man standing beside them. He was staring up at the screen with shock, relief and rage all dancing over his face – and he had bright eyes and baggy red pants.

'You're Nim's dad!' shouted Erin.

'Who's Nim?' asked the twins.

The television showed Selkie porpoising around Nim and Alex's kayak.

'Our friend!' Erin and Ben said together.

'You're Erin?' exclaimed Jack.

'And Ben,' said Ben.

'Tell me everything!' said Jack.

The camera showed the Professor pointing accusingly. It narrowed in on the tranquilliser gun at his side.

'That's the man who seal-napped Selkie!'

'And the other animals and birds.'

'Nim didn't mean to stow away – she was trying to rescue Selkie!'

'We've got to help!'

'Police have been called to recapture the animal,' said the reporter.

Jack ran towards the Exit sign.

'Wait!' shouted Mr Caritas. 'I'll come with you!'

'We all will,' said Mrs Caritas.

They raced together through the airport to the long line of yellow taxis parked outside. Jack jumped into the first one with Erin, Ben and their dad, and Mrs Caritas and the twins grabbed the one behind.

'This is an emergency,' said Jack. 'To the kayak pier – as fast as you can!'

'The one on the news?' asked the driver. 'With the sea lion?'

'Yes. Please hurry!'

'Gotcha!' said the driver, and pulled out so fast they were knocked back in their seats.

The taxi zigzagged and zipped through the freeway traffic. Jack closed his eyes so he didn't have to see the scenery blurring past, and listened hard to Erin and Ben telling him what had happened on the ship. His face was white; sometimes he looked angry and sometimes he groaned – but sometimes he smiled.

'Nim's never had a kid friend before,' he said at last. 'She's very lucky to have met you two.'

'We like her,' said Erin.

'We've never met anyone like her,' said Ben.

'I can believe that,' said Jack.

They told him about seeing Alex in the morning, and his face grew even paler and sadder, and he didn't say anything at all.

'Why didn't you tell your mum and me about this before?' Mr Caritas asked.

'We were afraid…'

'Because the Professor said he'd put Nim in jail!'

'That's not going to happen!' their father and Jack said together.

They crossed a bridge to reach the city. The taxi honked and blared its way through the traffic and down to the pier. They could see the masts of sailing boats, and a crowd of people gathered on the shore.

Jack handed a wad of money to the driver, leapt from the cab and ran.

A policeman stopped him. 'Whoa! Stop right there. We've got a wild animal loose.'

'But that's my daughter!' said Jack. 'The girl, not the sea lion. The sea lion's her friend. They've grown up together.'

'And the woman?'

'She's…' said Jack. 'Well, she used to be…I mean, I know who she is but I don't know if…'

'I see,' said the policeman. 'But the gentleman over there informs me that the animal is extremely dangerous if approached by untrained people, so I can't let you past.'

'That *gentleman*,' said Jack, his face turning scarlet with fury, 'is a wildlife poacher. Search his ship and you'll find other animals that need to be rescued. *He's* the only dangerous animal here.'

The Professor hadn't noticed Jack. He strode over to the policeman. 'We can't wait any longer – that animal needs to be got back into captivity. I'll shoot it with a tranquilliser dart.'

'You're not going to tranquillise that sea lion!' said Jack.

'Everybody keep calm!' said the policeman to the Professor. Because Erin and Ben, their mother and father and the twins had snuck behind the crowd to where the kayaks were kept. They were now paddling in tight circles around Selkie.

More people from the crowd followed, until every kayak on the pier was surrounding Selkie, blocking her from the Professor.

A reporter pushed his way up to the policeman, followed by a man in a chauffeur's uniform. 'This man says he drove the sea lion down here in his limousine, and it wasn't dangerous at all.'

'I'll second that!' said Carla, racing across the lawn with Fritz at her heels. 'She doesn't even squash cakes!'

'I don't know if she belongs to anyone,' said Daniel, 'but I know she loves that little girl, and that Nim loves her.'

'And I think you'll find,' said Ivan, 'that this is the wildlife poacher I reported to the police earlier today.'

'What do you say to all that?' the reporter demanded, shoving his microphone in the Professor's face.

'I say I'm getting that animal back!' shouted the Professor.

'Put the gun down!' shouted the policeman.

The Professor ignored him, and raised his dart gun.

Jack sprang at him.

The policeman sprang too.

Jack and the policeman clunked heads, and their heads clunked the Professor's arm.

'Ow!' screamed the Professor, as the tranquilliser dart jabbed his leg. 'Ooh,' he moaned as the injection went in. He slumped down, and was asleep before the policeman's handcuffs clamped around his arm.

Jack ran across the grass faster than he'd ever run. He dived into the water and swam straight out. Selkie honked her happiest honk as she dived towards him.

'Jack!' Nim shouted.

'Jack!' Alex whispered.

They reached for him – and their kayak tipped over.

The three of them clung to the upside-down kayak, laughing and hugging, exclaiming and explaining, till Fred poked his face up between them, and Selkie honked anxiously that they needed to get back to shore.

'You're right, Selkie,' said Jack. 'I think it's time for us all to go home.'

'All of us?' asked Nim.

'All of us,' said Alex.

Chapter 23

THERE WERE TOO many things to organise to go back to
the island right away. 'Besides,' said Nim, 'there's a lot to
see in the city!'

So while Jack and Nim went to talk to the police about
the Professor, Alex went to see the boat that looked like a
cottage, and rented it for two weeks. Selkie and Fred liked
it because they could get on and off into the river any time
they wanted, and stay home by themselves when Nim, Jack
and Alex did things they didn't want to do. Nim, Jack and
Alex liked it because when they got back from a busy day
in the busy city they could breathe the fresh air and sit
peacefully to watch the sun setting over the river.

They went to museums and saw dinosaurs and tiny
fossils, Egyptian mummies and suits of armour, enormous
paintings and miniature carvings. They went to a library
with paintings on the ceilings and stone lions outside the
doors. They walked through the hot city streets and into
chilled stores where they bought shoes and clothes, and
where women sprayed perfume that made Jack sneeze.
They went to a cinema and forgot to eat their popcorn

because the screen was so big and the sound so all around them that they felt as if they were in the story too. They ate bagels and hot dogs and foods Nim had never heard of; they had afternoon tea at the hotel that looked like a palace, and rode through the streets in the carriage behind the horse called Mabel. They had a party with all their friends and an iguana-shaped cake that made Fred sneeze with surprise.

But best of all was the hot, hot day they all went to the huge park in the middle of the city. The taxi drove down a gently curving road and dropped them off where a path led to a tranquil green lake. When the driver opened the door, Selkie galumphed half way down the path before he could even say, 'Here we are!'

'I didn't know sea lions could move so fast!' said the driver. 'Or *him*.'

Fred was racing behind Selkie as fast as his short iguana legs would carry him.

People jumped off the path out of their way, dogs barked, and Selkie and Fred slid into the water.

A row of turtles sunning on a log slowly turned their heads to stare, and one by one, disappeared under the water.

Fred came up from the bottom with a grin full of water plants.

Selkie popped up halfway across the lake to check if she could still see Nim. A gold fish tail stuck out of the side of her mouth.

Then one by one, the dogs jumped in and paddled after Selkie and Fred, splashing and barking in the craziest, splashingest game of coconut-soccer-without-a-coconut that ever was.

Their families laughed as they watched them.

Other families wandering through the park came to watch, too.

And Nim, Alex and Jack watched and laughed too, and sat on the bank together for the rest of the afternoon.

P.S.

From: nim@kidmail.com
To: erin@kidmail.com, ben@kidmail.com
Date: Thursday July 22, 10:05am
Subject: Home on the island

Dear Erin and Ben

   I told you I'd write again as soon as we got back to
the island. The city was fun but I'm really happy I'm
home now.

   Our trip back was very different. This captain let
Selkie and Fred have their own pool, and I slept in
a cabin. It was a lot more comfortable, but I missed
doing things with you. Once we saw a whale spouting
and I wished you could have seen it too. We stopped at
different places to take the smuggled animals back to
their homes.

   We bought a new sailboat when we got to Sunshine
Island so we could sail the rest of the way. Jack was
going to build our new boat but Alex said this was a
present from her book, and Jack said okay because he
wanted us all to be home again as fast as possible.

Selkie swam most of the way, which was good because she took up all the deck when she had a nap, and also she liked showing the dolphins around, because they decided to follow us home. So did some of the birds.

Jack says the Professor and the Troppo Captain should stay in jail a long, long time. I hope so. So do Kylie, Kelvin and Kristie. They visited us at the houseboat and said how upset they felt when they found out about the animal smuggling. They're going to work on another boat now and Virginia is going to work in a zoo to help the animals who need to learn how to be free after being in cages for too long.

Did you see I have my own email address now so you can write to me as much as you want. But the best thing is that Jack and Alex said I can invite you to come and stay with us on the island next summer. I hope you'll come.

Love (as much as Selkie loves Fred)

Nim

WENDY ORR was born in Canada and spent her childhood across Canada, France and the USA. Wherever she lived, there were always lots of stories, books and pets.

Once, when she was on a ferry going to visit her grandparents, Wendy saw a tiny island and wished that she could live there. As soon as she got home, she started writing a story about a girl who runs away from an orphanage to live on a small island. Many years later, when she was a grown-up writer, Wendy remembered the feeling of writing that story, and started writing *Nim's Island*.

Wendy began writing for children after a career as an occupational therapist. She is the author of many award-winning books and lives on Victoria's Mornington Peninsula.

One day a film producer in Hollywood took Wendy's book *Nim's Island* out of the library to read to her son. The next day she asked if she could make it into a movie. Wendy said yes! They became good friends, and Wendy had the fun of helping work on the screenplay. A second film followed, called *Return to Nim's Island*.

~

KERRY MILLARD was born in Canada and grew up surrounded by all sorts of animals, including a monkey. One day Kerry took her crazy dog to dog school, drew some cartoons for their newsletter, and accidentally began a new career as an award-winning cartoonist and illustrator, and author.